MW01528840

# SYSTEMA PARADOXA

ACCOUNTS OF CRYPTOZOOLOGICAL IMPORT

VOLUME 27
GHOST OF THE DAWNLANDS
A TALE OF THE SKADEGAMUTC

AS ACCOUNTED BY ROBERT E. WATERS

NEOPARADOXA
Pennsville, NJ
2025

PUBLISHED BY
NeoParadoxa
A division of eSpec Books
PO Box 242
Pennsville, NJ 08070
www.especbooks.com

ISBN: 978-1-956463-89-7
ISBN (ebook): 978-1-956463-88-0

Interior Design: Danielle McPhail
www.sidhenadaire.com

Cover Art: JW Harp
Cover Design: Mike and Danielle McPhail, McP Digital Graphics
Interior Illustration: JW Harp

Copyediting: Greg Schauer and John L. French

# DEDICATION

To all the Wabanaki Tribes
of Maine and Canada

# PROLOGUE

*Millinocket, Maine, 1988*

He brought the woman to his home because she was dying.

A woman in her seventies, overweight with ashen skin, suffering from Alzheimer's and diabetes, liver disease, and swollen ankles. The lady was scheduled to go into hospice care, but as her primary physician, he had told her family about how to keep her swelling down and her A1C to a minimum. He had promised them that she would *not* die; not soon, at least. He then took her to Operating Room 1 and said that he would "take care of her." That was a lie. Instead, he slipped out of the hospital's emergency exit, put her in his SUV, and brought her to his house. And here, at his home, she would die peacefully.

The man parked the car in his garage and closed the door. She was moaning on the stretcher, some incoherent gibberish that he tried to decipher. She was Wabanaki, a Native American tribe from Maine, speaking the Abenaki language. The man understood the language, being a member of the Penobscot tribe himself, but she was whispering too low for him to hear.

"Do not fret, Mary," he said, smiling at her. "You will be at peace soon. I promise."

Climbing out of his SUV, he opened the hatchback. There she was, on a stretcher in her hospital gown, a PICC line of sedatives in her hand, making her comfortable.

The man pulled the stretcher out and put his arms underneath her back and legs to carry her into his home. As he picked her up, she moaned. Mary was heavy, but he was a strong wizard of the Penobscot tribe. The man could handle her weight and the incoherent words drooling out of her mouth.

He kicked open his door and took her inside. There wasn't much time for the ritual, for he had to move fast (they were coming). He put her on the table in his ceremonial room. There, she would find peace and comfort. She opened her eyes and looked at him. "What… what are you doing, doctor?"

"Taking care of you," he said, with a polite smile and nod. "Do not worry, sweet Mary. You will be at peace soon."

He had brought other patients to his home: a woman in her twenties who had OD'd on cocaine and had fallen into a coma; a man who had broken his spine from a terrible fall, and a young boy with leukemia. All of them had been his patients at the Millinocket Regional Hospital, where he had been a surgeon for ten years, but they would not survive, including the woman he had in his arms right now. The man knew it instinctively. He could see their futures and knew that their pain would not subside, that their suffering would be acute and unrelenting. So, why not bring them home and end it all right here? It was the right — the *practical* — thing to do.

Lying her on the table, she tried stopping him, tried pushing his hands away, but the sedatives in her PICC line kept her groggy and weak. "Peace, Mary," he said as he settled her down and strapped her arms and legs to the table. He stroked her dark hair and touched her face. He kissed her forehead. "I am going to take care of you. Now, close your eyes and breathe deeply."

The woman closed her eyes and breathed. In the distance, he heard the swirling riot of sirens drawing closer. *Damn!* Oh, how he wished that he could wrap her in birch bark as Wabanaki tradition dictated. He had done so with the other three patients now buried in his backyard; he would love to bury her respectfully, several feet deep as well, but the sirens were too loud, and too distracting. The only thing that he could do with her was drive a knife into her chest. One clean and simple thrust before *they* arrived.

*Get it done.*

He had a pistol on the small of his back, beneath his belt. When the time came, he would use it, but for now, all that mattered was Mary. The woman deserved peace and freedom.

Picking up the knife, he placed it on the tray beside the table. A long, thin knife, serrated edge, sharp and ready. Mary still had her eyes closed; perhaps she was asleep. That was best because it meant that he would be able to conduct the ceremony quickly and efficiently.

He turned the knife so that the tip pointed toward Mary's chest. Saying ceremonial words in Abenaki. He talked about *Wulastegniak*, the "good river people." He spoke of the St. John's River, and how lovely the water flowed down the river. And surprisingly, despite her closed eyes, she recited them as well, quietly mimicking his words as she squirmed against the straps. Mary smiled, and a warm sensation filled his chest. He knew now that she accepted her death in full. A tear fell from her eye. A tear fell down his face as well.

He could hear the police cars sliding to a stop in his driveway, sirens still blaring. Hearing their footsteps and movements toward the house. *Do it now... now!* he thought and raised the knife again.

The door burst open, and several officers rushed in, screaming, shouting, yelling. He paused, the blade inches from her chest. He looked at her, her face pale, her mouth open. Her eyes were open as well, and he suddenly realized that he no longer needed to drive the blade into her chest.

Mary was already dead.

The officers swarmed into his ceremonial room. "Lucas Maske... keep your hands up!" several shouted. "Hands in the air!"

Doing as they ordered, he moved away from the table. "It's okay, gentlemen." He pointed to Mary. "I did not kill her. She died on her own."

"On the ground!" They shouted again. "Hands behind your head!"

He realized now that he could not tolerate their demands. He was a Penobscot wizard and magician, and how dare they declare that his acts of "euthanasia" were criminal? How *dare* they? *I'm a saint, a liberator. I save people from their suffering!*

As directed, he bent his knees and fell to the floor. Then, he reached for his pistol, drew it, and pulled the trigger. He fired three rounds before they opened fire.

He dropped, several bullets striking his chest, stomach, and shoulders. *I will not die!* he said to himself as blood flowed from his body. *I will not die! I am a Penobscot wizard. I cannot die!*

And so, he did not. When they placed his shattered shell in a body bag and on a stretcher and the coroners carried him to the ambulance, a small ball of light rose out of the bag and flew up into the night sky. The ball of light grew larger and larger, and in time, it drifted into the dense canopy of trees above his home. In the middle of the ball of light was the magician's face, staring down at his corpse and the officers who had killed him.

But, he was not dead, and he was happy about that. For it meant that he would continue to live and continue to do good deeds for the Wabanaki people.

He smiled and laughed. The ball of light drifted deep into the Maine forest and disappeared.

# CHAPTER ONE

*Maine, 2024, Near Moosehead Lake*

Joe Littlecloud and his assistant, Horus Ruth, had the Skadegamutc cornered. They were happy about that, though having the
beast trapped in a deserted barn wasn't the most ideal situation.
Too many cracks and crevasses in the wood planks. Too many
wide-open gaps in the ceiling. Too many shattered doors. Luckily,
the creature was in human form. Thin, tall, and emaciated, yes,
but human, nonetheless. More like a zombie, really, with dark
grey skin, infinite wrinkles, and long, thick black hair. They had
it cornered in the midnight hour, with torches in hand. All that
remained was to kill it.

The Skadegamutc snarled and hissed. It lashed out at Littlecloud with sharp, piercing claws. It gnashed its teeth and ducked
as Horus Ruth tried dousing it with gasoline. The gas flew over
the creature, striking the wall.

Ruth cursed. "Gah! It's too nimble," he said, dropping the
gasoline canister and shifting his torch to his other hand. "Too
quick. I don't think we'll be able to—"

"Nonsense," Littlecloud said. "Keep your eye on it, Horus, and
don't let it flee."

The Skadegamutc had been terrorizing Maine and parts of
Canada for decades, far longer than any other Native American
cryptid in the United States had done. Why, then, in all the world,
hadn't the FBI-VPA taken steps to find and destroy this...
monstrosity? Littlecloud had no answer for that.

"Run away from me," the Skadegamutc hissed as it moved
toward a large gap in the barn wall. "Flee, or you will both die!"

"I hardly think that is an option," Littlecloud said, trying to punch the creature with his torch. "You are in human form, Lucas. You cannot escape us."

The Skadegamutc chuckled, a low, guttural chuckle that troubled Littlecloud. "Can't I?"

Littlecloud blinked, and suddenly, his mind was aswirl with memories of his past. Old memories. Bad memories. Memories of his alcohol and spousal abuse, of his constant anger, of his youthful arrogance and overconfidence. He fell to the barn floor and fought to pull away from these thoughts, but the Skadegamutc's mind was too powerful, too relentless in its cognitive functions. It had the ability to divine its enemies' emotional distress and then focus on those emotions to drive its opponents mad.

"Sir," Ruth said, placing his free hand on Littlecloud's shoulder. "Are you all right?"

The memories of him slapping his former wife in a fit of rage flashed in his mind. Littlecloud shuddered and let a tear drop from his eye. "Kill it," he said, pushing out a squeak. "Kill it *now*, Horus."

Horus Ruth threw the torch on the floor near the Skadegamutc's feet. He then picked up the gas canister and tried splashing the creature, but the Skadegamutc moved, raised its arm, slamming its fist against Ruth's face and knocking him back.

"Horus," Littlecloud shouted, his gut tied in knots. "No!"

Ruth slid across the barn floor, his face bloody, his body disheveled. He seemed unconscious.

Littlecloud tried standing, tried tossing his torch at the Skadegamutc, hoping to set it aflame, but the creature, again, dodged the torch and blinked its eyes.

It then shifted into a ball of light, illuminating the barn, casting shadows on the far wall. Littlecloud covered his face to shield his eyes from the intense glare. The creature chuckled again, dropped another terrible memory in Littlecloud's mind, and then slipped through the gap in the barn wall.

It was gone. It took Littlecloud several minutes to recover from his painful memories. He then crawled to his assistant.

Already he barely recognized Ruth's face. Beneath a sheen of blood, his features swelled, his nose misshapen. Shattered, Littlecloud would say, based on the radiating discoloration and Ruth's swollen blackened eyes. A couple blood-coated teeth lay in the dust beside him. "Oh, my poor, poor boy."

Littlecloud reached into his pocket and pulled out his cell phone. He called 911 and gave them his location. He then placed his phone back in his pocket, leaned over his assistant, and stroked his head. "I'm so sorry, Horus."

"It's okay, sir," Ruth said, blood streaming down his face. He tried sitting up, only to sway and lay back down. "We did our best."

For the third time. The embarrassment for Littlecloud was too much to bear.

He had tracked this Skadegamutc for years. More than once he and Ruth had cornered it but failed to take it out. Littlecloud had not thought that this time, here in this barn, the creature would be able to resist. So weak and feeble it was, due to its lack of ingesting blood, that even the idea of it reminding Littlecloud of his terrible past could not even be considered. It had been a while since the beast had feasted on human flesh. It was weaker now, but not powerless.

"What now, sir?" Ruth asked, holding a handkerchief hard against his nose to staunch the bleeding. "How do we find it again?"

Littlecloud leaned back, crossed his legs, and considered. *Indeed, what do we do now?* How would they find this Skadegamutc a fourth time and, finally, kill it? How indeed?

An idea came to him. At first, he rejected it. Then, he thought about it some more, and more, until it was clear that, perhaps, it was the only way to, once and for all, vanquish this hideous cryptid of the Wabanaki tribes.

"We need Chimalis Burton," Littlecloud said, nodding in confidence. "We need her... and her ceremonial knife."

# Chapter Two

*Aspen, Colorado*

Chimalis Burton watched the black Chevy Malibu pull into her driveway. At first, she thought it was FBI-VPA agents coming to tell her that her administrative leave had ended and that she was back in action. Her heart raced as she imagined how wonderful that would be: hunting down Native American cryptids again. What joy such an event would give her. Then, the car door opened, and a man climbed out.

"Damn!"

She liked this man and admired his skills in the field, but his arrogance and intransigence always got him into trouble with the Bureau. His hair was dark, long, and tied into a ponytail. His face carried grey stubble. He wasn't smiling, so Chimalis could tell that something grave, something troubling, brought him to her.

She opened the door and stared at him. She rolled her eyes. "Well, well, well. Joe Littlecloud. As I live and breathe. What the *hell* are you doing here?"

He walked up her steps and put out his hand. When she ignored the gesture a wry smile touched his lips and he lowered his arm. "Nice to see you again, too, Chimalis. It's been a long time."

Joe was an Apache shaman, a di-yin, who had conducted many rituals within his community. He was well-respected for such practices, though his youthful past was—to put it mildly—sketchy.

"I don't recall you ever paying me a visit. So, I'll ask again: why are you *here*?"

His expression soured. With a sniff, he wiped a little sweat from his brow and backed away. "I need your help, Chimalis. There's an important matter I'm trying to take care of. A cryptid matter in Maine. I'm… having some difficulty resolving it." His eyes dipped away, avoiding hers, and his jaw tightened. "I need your help."

Chimalis nodded. "I understand, but I'm sure you are aware that I have been placed on administrative leave. The Denver office of the FBI is investigating the killings of federal agents during my and Luiz's pursuit of the Qalupalik in Alaska. They believe that I may have been responsible for those deaths."

Chimalis looked at her arms. She had goosebumps. The thought of her in the water, the phobia that made her nervous and anxious was the reason she couldn't deal with water. It frightened her.

Joe nodded. "Yes, I'm very much aware of that. But you had nothing to do with those killings, Bluebird. Those sons of bitches at the VPA need to get their heads out of their asses and find you innocent of all charges. You don't deserve this."

"Perhaps," she said, feeling appreciative of his comment, "but until they decide if I'm guilty or not, I'm on leave. So, I'm afraid I cannot help you at this time, Joe."

Joe smiled and stepped toward Chimalis once more. "Well, Ms. Burton, I have some good news. I've spoken to your boss, SAC Halsey, and he's agreed to allow you to come with me to Maine to be my assistant."

"*What?*" She couldn't believe what she was hearing.

He stepped past her and into the house. "Come," he said, "we've got a lot to talk about."

She watched him walk into her living room and sit on the couch. *The nerve of the bastard!* As he crossed his legs, Chimalis considered grabbing her ceremonial knife and plunging it into his back. But no.

Not only would the bureau frown on her actions, but Joe Littlecloud was a shapeshifter, and a big one. If she were to stab him, her knife would undoubtedly crack and be destroyed.

Instead, she breathed deeply, trying to control her rage. She closed the door and walked into her living room. "Okay, Joe," she said, sitting across from him, her glare fixed on his worried face. "Tell me what's going on."

⌇

"I've been in pursuit of the Skadegamutc for three years now," he said, leaning forward. "You are familiar with that cryptid, yes?"

She nodded. Its name was pronounced "skuh-deh-guh-mooch," and she had known of Joe's pursuit of it for quite some time. She knew exactly what it was, but Joe described it anyway.

"The creature's name is Lucas Maske. He was a chief surgeon at the Millinocket Regional Hospital in Maine for ten years in the '70s and '80s. He was also a Penobscot magician and sorcerer of the Wabanaki Confederacy." Joe swallowed, and Chimalis could see his throat move up and down. He seemed agitated. "He... used to bring near-death patients to his home and euthanize them. He did this several times until the police finally figured it out. They cornered him in his home as he was trying to kill his final patient, a Mary Breckinridge, if I'm not mistaken. He pulled a pistol and shot three of them, but they too returned fire. Multiple shots. All kill shots."

"Well," Chimalis said, raising her hands, "if he is dead —"

"He's not dead," Joe said, cutting her off with a swift wave of his hand. "Like all Wabanaki sorcerers, he *refused* to die. His body was shattered, indeed, and buried, but his soul, his spirit, flew out of his corpse and into the woods, where he now exists as a Skadegamutc."

He paused, breathed deeply, and continued. "The Wabanaki call the Skadegamutc a Ghost-Witch. It exists in two different forms: as a human-like zombie with vampiric tendencies, feasting on the flesh of human beings, and drinking their blood. At night, it also exists as a ball of light, moving through the woods and various communities, preying upon people by drawing attention to their foul deeds and sorrow. The people become traumatized. He then comforts them, draws them in, learns of their terrible behavior, and then, as I said, feasts upon them by drawing energy and strength out of their bodies.

"This is a creature that has terrorized Maine and Canada for decades, Chimalis. It has shattered hundreds of lives. It *must* be destroyed, and I need your help finding it."

Chimalis leaned back in her chair and sighed deeply. She shook her head. "You realize how unethical it was for you to go to my boss and convince him to let me be your assistant? With all due respect, Joe, I don't answer to you. You're just a consultant, not an official VPA agent. You had no right to speak to Halsey."

"*Hundreds* of lives, Chimalis," Joe said, growing annoyed as he always did. "Many Wabanaki and American families devastated by its horrific actions. Given your background with trauma, I would think that you'd want to kill it."

Chimalis hesitated, trying to remain calm. His statement was insulting, though, given his violent past, she understood his tit-for-tat response. Like him, she had suffered great: her wild, uncontrollable emotions fighting against *El Cadejo*, the death of her fiancé against Mapuche demons in South-Central Chile, her high school friend's devastating injury during a swimming accident in Colorado. Those events had affected Chimalis emotionally, but Joe Littlecloud's past was even worse.

In his twenties, he'd been an abuser and an alcoholic. He had been condemned by a Mescalero Apache shaman who had driven him out of their community by making him a shapeshifter, twisting his body into a brown bear. His behavior now was... respectable, though he still had a level of arrogance that troubled her.

"Don't you have an assistant?" she asked. "A guy named Horus Ruth?"

Joe rubbed his eyes as if he were about to cry. "In our last confrontation with the Skadegamutc, in a barn near Moosehead Lake, Horus was badly damaged. His nose was shattered, his jaw cracked. He's not able to serve me anymore, at least not right away." He stood straight and flashed a meek smile. "He's in the hospital, and he'll be staying there for a couple weeks. That's why I need you, Chimalis. You and your knife."

Chimalis looked toward her fireplace. Her knife was on the mantel, resting comfortably in its sheath. It was a Zuni ceremonial blade that her mother had given her when Chimalis had officially become a VPA agent. And, according to her mother, the knife had been forged by the Zuni twin gods of war, Ahayu'da. The gods of war themselves had been created by Awonawilona, the Sun God. Mother had always been a little hazy on exactly when and why Ahayu'da had forged the blade, and for what purpose. In truth, Chimalis had always chalked up the legend to myth and hearsay, handed down generation to generation until the blade finally, for some unknown reason, landed in her possession. One thing was true, though: the knife had the power to vanquish cryptid lifeforces, and it was a critical part of her ability to serve as a VPA agent. She couldn't imagine functioning as an agent without her knife.

Chimalis stood and walked over to the fireplace. She reached for the knife and held it firmly. Unsheathing it, she carefully rubbed the blade with her fingers. It was sharp and warm. She looked at the myriad symbols on the blade of the cryptids that she had vanquished during her time in the VPA. The three most significant symbols were the Atasaya, the El Cadejo and the Qalupalik. Other symbols were etched there as well, multiple Native American cryptids that she had had the pleasure of destroying to save the lives of so many people. She was proud of her knife.

"May I see it?" Joe asked. Chimalis nodded and handed it to him.

He held it delicately in his hands, moving his thumb up and down the blade. He gazed at the symbols, cracked a smile, and said, "This blade *will* kill the Skadegamutc. I guarantee it." He handed it back to her. "I apologize for going to your boss and asking for you to be my assistant, but it was necessary. Horus Ruth is out. I need your help.

"You are Zuni, not Wabanaki or Algonquin, so perhaps you're not aware of their culture, but you are one of the best VPA agents in the world. You and your knife have vanquished so many cryptids in this world — the most, in fact. You're the best, Bluebird. There's no one else who has more knowledge and skill in destroying cryptids than you do."

Joe stood, smiled, and put his hand on her shoulder. "So, what do you say: will you help me? I need to save Maine from that vile beast."

He was buttering her bread, for sure. She wasn't against it. It made her feel good being praised for her dedication to the VPA. She did, indeed, have unique knowledge and skills when it came to cryptids. And, of course, her knife gave her an edge.

Chimalis chuckled and shook her head. "You are one arrogant piece of work, Joe, but you are good at what you do... most of the time, anyway." She nodded. "Okay, I'll play along. I'll come to Maine with you. But let's be clear on one thing."

Joe waited patiently for her to speak. "Yes?"

"Don't you go bossing me around."

# CHAPTER THREE

*Portland, Maine*

Niben Bellerose allowed the Skadegamutc to drink blood from her arm. It was something that he had performed frequently, with patience. Slow, steady sips, not deep, life-fulfilling gulps like he had done to other human beings in Maine. Niben had no fear that he would kill her. She was important to his survival.

She sat in a chair in her home while the creature knelt beside her, his long, dark, and messy hair hanging over her lap like Spanish Moss. His sharp teeth pierced her flesh and punctured the vein. She could hear him feeding. She did not like it. She hated him, wanted to kill him, but she was powerless. As his thrall, there was nothing she could do to keep him from drinking her blood and reveling in her youthful energy.

"You must find a way to kill Joe Littlecloud," the Skadegamutc said. As he removed his mouth from her arm blood dripped on her lap. "He and his foul assistant almost killed me in the barn. I cannot allow him to try that again. I must live... forever. You understand that?"

The creature put his mouth back on her arm and drank once more.

Like the Skadegamutc, Niben was a member of the Penobscot tribe. She was also a member of the FBI-VPA. For years she had given her friend Joe Littlecloud false information, leading him astray in his investigation of the creature that now knelt beside her, feasting on her arm. With his assistant Horus Ruth, Joe had almost burned the creature to ash in that barn. In truth, she wished he'd succeeded.

Back in the 1950s and '60s, there had been reports of two other Skadegamutc doing evil work in Maine and Canada, but both of them had suffered terrible destruction through fire. Unfortunately, this monster before her, lapping her arm, had lived for decades. A sadness insurmountable.

The Skadegamutc pulled his mouth away from her arm again, lifted his head, and exposed bloody teeth. "Did you hear what I said?"

"Yes, sir."

The creature finished his feeding. Sitting back, he licked his lips. Niben placed a rag on her arm and pressed it down. She felt weak, tired, and despite his desire not to see her die, he had drawn more blood from her now than he had on previous visits. It was clear to Niben that the Skadegamutc was desperate to drink blood and feed on human flesh. The VPA in Maine had given strict warnings to its citizenry, guidelines that would ensure their safety against this ghost-witch, this vampire who roamed the state seeking victims. He was not the same monster that he had been years ago. His search for victims was becoming more difficult, more problematic, and with Joe Littlecloud on the case, the Skadegamutc grew increasingly frustrated and increasingly weaker.

He was looking at her now, his lips red, his deep eyes staring into her worried face. In her mind, the creature could easily draw upon her past emotional crisis, terrifying her, just like he had done to Littlecloud recently.

She lowered her head in supplication, her hand pressing the rag into her arm. "I will continue to misdirect Joe Littlecloud, as you so order. But..."

"What?" The Skadegamutc asked. "Tell me, Niben."

"There's a new VPA agent arriving here in Portland soon. Her name is... Chimalis Burton. She is Zuni — well, part Zuni, part British — and she is considered one of the best Native American agents in the country."

The Skadegamutc crawled to Niben and hovered over her like a hulking gorilla. She could smell his foul breath and his body odor, see his thin, floppy grey-skin arms waving back and forth like a rope bridge across a ravine. His lips were so close to hers, they almost kissed. She wanted to vomit, wanted to grab his throat and rip it out, but his stare was too intimidating, too awful to try.

"Tell me everything about her."

She told him what she knew of Chimalis and the number of Native American cryptids that she had vanquished. She spoke about Chimalis' ceremonial knife, tried to describe it as best she could, giving the Skadegamutc as many details as possible about how the blade was used, how it subsumed cryptids and kept them contained inside its blade forever. She spoke most recently about Chimalis' service in Alaska and how she had killed a Qalupalik with said knife. Finally, she told him about the investigation into the deaths of many FBI agents in Alaska, how Chimalis was on administrative leave and how she was being investigated for illegal activity, despite the fact that she was on her way to Maine.

"I do not know why she has been allowed to come here," Niben said, "but nevertheless, she is coming as Joe Littlecloud's assistant. She is... formidable."

The Skadegamutc shrieked, backed away, stood, and wandered through her living room. He stared at paintings on her walls and the photographs of the Thoreau-Wabanaki Trail Festival held annually in Maine. Niben had been to the festival many times, and that was where she had first met this creature, when he had invaded her mind with harmful memories of her troubled youth and of her abusive father. At the festival, he had come to her, comforted her, told her that everything was going to be all right. And then he sunk his fangs into her throat, and...

The Skadegamutc lifted his arms, spoke a few words in Abenaki, and then changed into a ball of light. Niben had seen him transform many times before. She was not afraid. She sat there, still and quiet, as the bright ball floated over to her.

It hovered above her face. "You will become good friends with this Chimalis Burton. You will take her into your home, give her food and companionship, and then—" the ball slowly drifted away toward an open window, "—you and I will kill her."

# CHAPTER FOUR

*Office of the FBI, Portland, Maine*

They arrived in Portland early, Chimalis greeting some of the staff.

"Thank you for allowing me to participate in this investigation," Chimalis said as she shook hands with three FBI agents.

"We're glad to have you here," Special-Agent-in-Charge Zack Berhard said. "Although, I must admit, our VPA staff is short. We have only one agent and two additional staff in charge of that organization."

*Hmm*, Chimalis thought. *Just like the VPA in Alaska. Always short-staffed.*

The agent in charge of Maine's VPA program was Niben Bellerose, and she stepped forward. She offered her hand and smiled. "Delighted to meet you, Agent Burton."

Chimalis shook her hand and nodded. She flashed a smile. "Delighted to meet you too, Agent Bellerose. I'm glad Maine has at least *one* agent in charge of the VPA."

There were a lot of members of the FBI that considered cryptid investigation to be... how could she put it... foolish and unnecessary. Thus, the budget for the VPA was usually small. Though luckily, not in Denver. Colorado had a strong, healthy VPA department. Chimalis was happy about that.

"You are Wabanaki, is that right?" Chimalis asked.

Niben nodded. "Yes. A member of the Penobscot tribe, in fact. I've been in service for the VPA for five years."

"And she has been critical in providing key information about the Skadegamutc." Joe smiled and put out his arms.

Joe and Niben greeted each other warmly with a kiss on the cheek and a strong hug, though Chimalis saw a small bit of apprehension in Agent Bellerose's eyes. She seemed uncomfortable hugging Littlecloud, as if she were worried about his well-being.

"Feel free to use the conference room to discuss the case." SAC Berhard motioned them to the room near the back of the office.

Joe nodded. "Of course. Thank you."

"Take all the time you need," he said before returning to his office.

As they sat at the long table, Agent Bellerose provided information about three of the most recent locations where the Skadegamutc had been seen.

"We'll go to those places," Joe said, laying out a map on the table, pointing to the three key locations, "and canvass those areas. That could give us information about where the beast is currently located."

"What about his old house?" Chimalis asked. "We could go there as well."

Joe shook his head. "The house was demolished about five years ago, and the bodies that he buried in his backyard were exhumed and given proper burials. So, there's really no reason to go there. It's all gone."

Chimalis nodded, and they continued to review the map. Other areas of significance were in and around lakes: Moosehead Lake, Webb Lake, and Sebago Lake. Those were places where the Skadegamutc had attacked before, several years back. "Webb and Sebago aren't significant in my opinion," Joe said. "Families in those areas were attacked decades ago, and it's unlikely that we'll discover anything of import if we go there. Moosehead Lake is key, however. The Thoreau-Wabanaki Trail Festival is held there annually. We should go and investigate the area."

"Absolutely," Niben said, turning to Chimalis. "The festival is the place to learn the Wabanaki culture. I'm sure you'd be interested in doing so."

Chimalis nodded. "Sure, let's start there."

As Joe took the map and folded it, Niben again turned to Chimalis. "And, as I understand it," Niben said, "you'll attempt to kill it with your knife?"

Chimalis nodded. "That's the plan, yes. Assuming I can approach it safely and stab it in its back. All it'll take is a puncture, and the blade will do its duty."

"That shouldn't be a problem," Joe said. "We'll attempt to corner it again, like Horus and I did in that barn, and then you'll stab it."

Chimalis huffed and rolled her eyes. She turned to Niben. "I know what the Skadegamutc is, but I'll do my best. It's my understanding, as Joe explained it to me, that this creature is one of the strongest, toughest Native American cryptids in existence."

"It is." Niben reached out and touched Chimalis' hand. She gently tapped it and smiled. "And it's *my* understanding that you are the best VPA investigator in the United States."

Chimalis reached out and touched Niben's hand as well. Looking down at Niben's arm Chimalis frowned, noticing scars on the agent's skin, light puncture wounds. "So I've been told, but let's concentrate on the Skadegamutc. Joe told me that this creature's original name was Lucas Maske, and that he was a Penobscot sorcerer and a doctor for several years."

Niben pulled her hand away. Standing, she pushed her chair back and ruffled through documents on the table. "Yes, that's correct." She handed some of the documents to Chimalis and sat back down. "His information is all in here."

Chimalis reviewed the documents. A doctor for ten years, as Joe had indicated. Also, a strong proponent of euthanasia, as the documents told of how he took patients to his home, killed them, and then conducted Wabanaki rituals upon their corpses. She then looked through the documents detailing his transformation into the Skadegamutc a ball of energy… a walking corpse of grey, and a bloodthirsty vampire, draining virtually every person that he had attacked. There were several accounts of this creature terrorizing dozens of families throughout Maine. The details of his violence were excruciating, almost overwhelming, to Chimalis as she gleaned through page after page. She felt uncomfortable.

"You're Penobscot too, correct?" Chimalis asked Niben.

"Yes. And a member of the Wabanaki Confederacy."

Chimalis looked at Joe and smiled. "I'd like Agent Bellerose to be part of our team."

Both Joe and Niben seemed surprised. Joe shook his head. "I don't think so."

"Why not?"

"Because she's the sole VPA agent in Portland. We can't risk her getting injured or killed by the Skadegamutc. Too risky."

Chimalis sighed. Once again annoyed with this Apache shaman. "Look... she's from the same tribe as Lucas Maske. She may not have had direct contact with the Skadegamutc, but she understands its connection with the Wabanaki." She looked at Niben. "She can provide better details about what the creature is, and how it behaves, than either you or I. Surely you agree with that."

Niben glanced at Joe, swallowed, then turned her attention to Chimalis. "Yes, it is true. I understand my people well. I can be of service, if you wish."

Chimalis waited until Joe finally sighed and said, "Fine. Niben, you'll be on our team. Meeting adjourned."

As they stood Chimalis asked Niben, "Do you know of a hotel nearby? I need to find a place to stay while I'm here."

"Why not stay with me?" Niben asked. She smiled. "My home's here in Portland, and I promise I won't charge you rent."

"Really?" Chimalis asked.

"Yes. And I can tell you all about my people, and maybe you'll have a better understanding of who the Wabanaki are, and thus, a better understanding of the Skadegamutc."

Chimalis could certainly benefit from more information about the Wabanaki. She had some knowledge of the culture, but not enough. She nodded. "Okay, I accept. And thank you, Agent Bellerose. I appreciate your assistance."

Niben walked up to Chimalis and gave her a light hug. "Please, call me Niben."

Chimalis squinted and looked up at the ceiling. "Doesn't Niben mean 'Summer Goddess'?"

"Yes," Niben said, surprised. "How did you know?"

Chimalis chuckled. "I have a really large library in my house."

# CHAPTER FIVE

*Near the Border of New Brunswick, Canada*

The Skadegamutc waited patiently behind a rotting log for the rabbit to move closer. The little bunny hopped toward him, nibbling on bits of grass and small flowers. Closer and closer and closer. It hopped underneath the log, and the Skadegamutc snatched it up, breaking its neck and ripping it open.

What a delight! The Skadegamutc sighed happily not only drinking its sweet blood but devouring its flesh as well. Though, in truth, the taste of a mere forest creature was nothing compared to the taste of human beings. Humans were his salvation, his life blood, and Niben Bellerose had the best-tasting blood. She was, in effect, his kindred spirit. They were from the same tribe, almost twins in a way. Oh, how he loved her blood. And yet, he could not feed from her arm anymore. Not now, anyway. That hideous agent, Chimalis Burton, was living with Niben. He had recommended it, of course, so that Niben could learn personal, emotional things about Chimalis and, in time, provide him with that information so that he could end her life. But, Niben was often weak on personal matters. She was — he hated to admit it — a *good* person. She would do her duty for him: give him information about Chimalis so that he could, in time, manipulate her thoughts, her dreams and desires. That was most necessary.

It was also necessary to manipulate hateful Joe Littlecloud's thoughts as well, for he had come so close, so many times, to killing him.

The combination of Agents Burton and Littlecloud sent a chill up the Skadegamutc's spine. Together, they could easily kill him, burn him to cinder, and scatter his ashes in the wind. The thought of that terrified him. *I cannot be killed,* he thought. *I am Skadegamutc! I must live forever.*

So, what to do now that two of the best FBI agents, and one consultant, were on the case?

He finished the rabbit and tossed it away. He wiped its blood from his mouth and sat down on the rotting log. He was thin and frail, so the wood did not splinter from his weight. He looked up into the canopy of trees and forced a smile. Maine was such a beautiful state. This was his place, his home, his sanctuary. He could not imagine being anywhere else.

And yet, he had to divert the agents' attention away from the grand work that he had done in Maine. He had to keep them out of the state so that he could feast upon all the good citizenry therein.

*I'll go to New Brunswick.*

Yes. That was where the Skadegamutc would go. He would find people there, draw their attention to all the hateful, hurtful memories of their past and bring them down.

He stood, licked more rabbit blood off his lips, shifted into a ball of light, and drifted toward the Canadian border.

*Niben Belleroses's House, Portland, Maine*

For dinner, Niben made a traditional Wabanaki meal for herself and Chimalis: hickory nut and hull corn salad, grilled whitefish, Three Sisters soup, and maple syrup pie. In truth, Chimalis would have preferred ordering pizza since she was *very* hungry, and it took quite a while for Niben's meal to be ready. Nevertheless, once they got down to business, Chimalis loved every bite.

"This is wonderful," she said, sipping her Three Sisters soup and taking a bite of her maple pie. "Some of the best I've had in a long time. Thank you."

They sat in Niben's living room, eating on the couch. Niben smiled and said, "Thanks. I'm glad you like it. The Wabanaki people love traditional Algonquin dishes. I enjoy making them."

"Oh, so you're technically Algonquin?"

Niben nodded. "Yes. The Wabanaki are Algonquin. We call ourselves 'The People of the Dawnlands. We are comprised of five nations: the Abenaki, the Mi'kmaq, the Maliseet, the Passamaquoddy, and the Penobscot. Our original territorial boundaries encompassed Maine, Vermont, New Hampshire, and many parts of Canada."

"Tell me about these tribes," Chimalis said, anxious to understand them all.

Niben nodded. "As you wish. The Maliseet call themselves the 'People of the Bright River', and their territory lies across the current borders of New Brunswick and Quebec and, of course, parts of Maine. Many live near the Saint John River. The Mi'kmaq reside primarily in the Northeastern Woodlands, Canada's Atlantic provinces, Nova Scotia, New Brunswick, and New-foundland.

"The Passamaquoddy live primarily in the Canadian province of New Brunswick and in Maine. The name literally means "pollock-spearer," which refers to the pollock fish, a significant food source for their people. The Abenaki, as I'm sure you're aware, derive their name from the Wabanaki, the 'People of the Dawnlands'. Ethnologists have classified them as two different groups: Western Abenaki and Eastern Abenaki. They too reside in Canada and Maine.

"And finally, the Penobscot, of which I am a member." Niben smiled, wiggled on the couch, and continued. "We call ourselves the 'People of Where the White Rocks Extend Out', and we live primarily along the Penobscot River within Maine. We are a federally-recognized tribe."

Chimalis nodded. "Good information. Thanks."

"You're welcome." Niben continued, with a less enthusiastic expression on her face. "In the 1500s and 1600s, the Wabanaki people were often enslaved by Europeans, which, I'm sure, was not unlike the Zunis."

Chimalis nodded. "Oh, yes. Back in the day, we fought the Spanish a lot. We won some of those battles and lost others.

Some of my people *were* enslaved, much to my chagrin. It was a mess."

Niben nodded. "And my people suffered a terrible pandemic between 1616 and 1619. It was called "The Great Dying." Between those years, about seventy to ninety percent of all Algonquins perished." Niben sighed. "And, of course, shortly thereafter, British settlers rolled through and took a lot of our land."

Chimalis could see disdain in Niben's eyes. Completely understandable, considering how many Algonquins had suffered from that terrible plague and the forceful British incursion. Yet, Chimalis felt a little uncomfortable, given the fact that her father had been British and a member of the MI-6. Like her mother, her father later became an agent for the VPA and served the Bureau with honor and distinction. She missed them both.

"But we've endured," Niben said, laying her plate on the coffee table and tapping her lips with a handkerchief to clean away a few pie crumbs. "All five nations have survived, and we are strong again."

"Yes. Just like the Skadegamutc."

Niben smiled apprehensively. "Yes." She swallowed, cleared her throat, and said in a whisper, "And may he die."

"He was a wizard, correct?" Chimalis asked, hoping to learn more about the cryptid from Niben's perspective. "Back before he shifted into a ball of light and disappeared?"

"He was a wizard *and* a magician and considered by many Wabanaki to be one of the best to have ever lived. He had skills unparalleled by any other wizard-magician in the tribe." Niben sipped her wine. She moved closer to Chimalis. "But, if I may ask, let's talk about your ceremonial knife, how it functions, how it works. Tell me about it."

Chimalis was a little apprehensive to do so, but... Niben had shared about the Wabanaki tribes.

*Very well.*

She told her the history of the knife, how it was forged by the gods, and how her mother had given it to her. She also told Niben about how both her mother and father had been members of the

FBI-VPA, and how they had died. Chimalis felt comfortable speaking to Niben. She was sweet, attentive, and seemed more than willing to assist in their pursuit of the creature.

"You mentioned earlier that you would stab the Skadegamutc in the back," Niben said, taking another drink of her wine, "but... can't you just stab it anywhere? You don't have to drive the knife into its back, do you?"

"The blade can pierce the flesh anywhere, yes." Chimalis said. "But, the blade must go in at least halfway for it to subsume the creature's spirit. Which means, of course, that it cannot simply pierce its hand or its foot. It must pierce the body, its back, its chest. It needs to puncture a substantial location on its body."

Niben seemed very excited about the information that Chimalis had given her. "And, you're the only one who can wield the knife, right? No one else can."

Chimalis shrugged and tilted her head to the left. "Well, not exactly. I'm its chief wielder, of course, but so long as the knife pierces the flesh of a Native American cryptid, anyone can use it."

"And it vanquishes the creature, yes? Subsumes its spirit? How does it do that, exactly?"

Chimalis was about to answer, but Niben's eyes were wide and inviting, as if she were begging for an answer. Instead, Chimalis leaned forward and set her wine glass down. She looked at her watch. "You know, it's nearly eleven o'clock. I think I'll go to bed, if that's okay with you. We have a lot of work to do tomorrow."

Niben put her wine glass down as well, seemed embarrassed, but smiled and stood up. "Sure, okay. That's best."

She offered Chimalis a hug. She accepted. "Good night, Niben. Again, it was a wonderful meal. You're a great cook!"

Niben chuckled. "My pleasure. And good night, Chimalis. I'm glad you're with us on this case. We couldn't defeat the beast without you."

Chimalis nodded. "Thanks. See you at seven."

Chimalis turned and walked into her room. She wanted to turn again and look at Niben but refrained. Chimalis scowled.

Niben had asked too many questions about her knife, about its use and functionality. Why?

Chimalis wasn't sure, but perhaps tomorrow, during their investigation of the Skadegamutc, she'd hopefully learn more about why Niben was so interested in her knife. Maybe.

*New Brunswick, Canada*

They were in their twenties, and he stared at them through their hotel window. They were happy, having just come from the casino on the first floor. They were on the seventh floor now, but that didn't matter to the Skadegamutc. He was a ball of light, hovering near their window, but keeping low so that they could not see him. Not yet, anyway.

He watched them enter the room. The two young women were holding onto their boyfriends. One fellow picked up his girlfriend and ran into the room. The other two simply walked in. In his ball of light, the Skadegamutc smiled. Such young, vibrant younglings.

*Ripe for feeding.*

He could hear them speak, talking about many different things: their winnings at the casino (small, yet sufficient), their return home in the morning, dirty jokes. One of the men was whistling a song. The Skadegamutc couldn't decipher the whistling, but that didn't matter. What mattered was their flesh and their blood. The most important thing was to pull those two agents out of Maine and into Canada, to divert their attention so that he could keep doing what he had done for decades in Maine: feed on the weary and the sorrowful. That mattered more than anything else.

He found a small gap in the window and flew into it. He was inside the wall now and closer to the four young people. That was significant, for being closer made it easier for him to divine their personalities and make them feel pain, anxiety.

They were kissing now, affirming their relationships and preparing for bed. There were two beds, and he knew that both couples would sleep in them and perhaps have sex. They didn't seem all that concerned with discretion. It didn't matter: they knew each other, and they were in love.

He started with one of the men, working into his mind, trying to find tiny moments of anxiety, and he found one. The man had been bullied as a child, for years, and the Skadegamutc focused his attention on those moments.

The guy pulled away from his girlfriend. "What's the matter?" she asked, rubbing his shoulder.

He shook his head. "I—I don't know. I'm suddenly remembering things from my past that... I'm sorry. I have to go to the bathroom."

The Skadegamutc then focused on one of the women. The oldest one, in her mid-twenties. When a child, she had leukemia, and she had almost died. The grief that her mother experienced, due to her daughter's cancer, was so great that she hadn't been able to go on. She mourned and cried for days, and considered killing herself, but she refrained. Her daughter survived, and her mother rejoiced.

Her boyfriend fell back in shock. "What the hell's wrong with you?" he asked.

"I'm—I'm—" She couldn't tell him, for the memories were too strong, too painful. "I'm sorry. I just remembered my mother's death when I was a little girl. I—I don't know why."

The Skadegamutc tried entering the minds of the other two, but their childhoods had been, unfortunately, pleasant. They did not suffer from any noteworthy anxiety or pain. That was a sadness, for the Skadegamutc wanted to make them *all* hurt, make them turn toward him so that he could comfort them, drain their blood, and eat their flesh.

He slid through another small gap in the windowpane and illuminated the room. The three in the room stared up, in awe, at the strong glowing ball.

"What the hell is *that*?" The man in the room asked.

The woman who hadn't vomited screamed, and the Skadegamutc flew through her body, smashing her stomach and entrails, cauterizing the wound from the heat of the light. She yelped and fell dead. The other woman screamed with tiny bits of vomit on her lips. She tried striking the ball of light, but the ball plowed through her arm and struck her chest, smashing her ribs and immolating her heart.

The Skadegamutc soared out of her body, hovered six feet above the floor, and shifted into human form. The man scrambled back, eyes wide and mouth open. He bumped into a table and a lamp fell. Grabbing it, he stood and pulled the cord out of the socket and held the lamp in front of him as a shield.

The other man, who was in the bathroom, came running out, fear and bewilderment in his eyes.

"Gentlemen," the Skadegamutc said, opening his hands as if he were Jesus. "Come to me, and I will absolve your pain."

They paused, then the one from the bathroom shouted, "You killed our girls!"

The Skadegamutc smiled and nodded. "I did. It was necessary. Now... come to me, and I will give you peace."

The one holding the lamp in front of him screamed, and tried slamming the lamp into the Skadegamutc. The lamp shattered into a dozen pieces. The blow didn't affect the creature at all. He pushed the broken lamp aside, grabbed the man by the throat, flashed his sharp teeth, and flung him across the room. The body struck the wall, breaking the plaster beneath the yellow wallpaper. The wallpaper ripped away, and the room shook, and his body contorted with twisted joints and broken bones. He fell to the floor, arms and leg twisted; his neck broken.

The Skadegamutc turned to the other man and held out his hands again. He smelled foulness, an aching stench. Clearly, he had shit in his pants. Nevertheless, the creature motioned for him. "Come, and all will be forgiven."

The man did not approach the Skadegamutc. Instead, girding his courage, he lashed out with balled fists and struck the creature three times in the face. The Skadegamutc was shocked at the temerity of the lad, though it hardly hurt. Such simple things like punches never affected him. He was invulnerable to such punishment.

Again, the Skadegamutc grabbed the man by the throat, pulled him close, and said, "I could have saved you." Bile rolled down his chin. "I could have saved you from your suffering. Now, it's too late."

He flung the man across the room, and he, too, struck the wall. Like the other one, he broke the plaster and tore the wallpaper, but this time, the body struck a beam inside the wall. The Skadegamutc heard the crack of the man's back. He fell to the floor, like the other, and was dead.

Now, there was quiet. The creature felt at peace. It was sad that neither man would come to him, that they had tried to defend themselves and their dead girlfriends. An honorable move, indeed, but foolish. Now, they were dead, and he had no other choice but to feed on them all.

He walked to the one who had held the lamp, fell to his knees, opened his mouth, and sunk his fangs into his throat.

*I will feed on every one of them*, the Skadegamutc thought as the warm blood coursed through his body, giving him an energy that he hadn't felt in a long time. *And Chimalis Burton and Joe Littlecloud will come.*

# CHAPTER SIX

The first location that they investigated was the barn where Joe and his assistant Horus were thwarted by the Skadegamutc. It was near Moosehead Lake, the place where the annual Thoreau-Wabanaki Trail Festival would be held. Joe absolutely wanted to attend the festival. Chimalis agreed to attend as well to get a better feel and understanding of the Wabanaki culture. Niben also agreed to attend, though she seemed a little apprehensive. Chimalis couldn't figure out why.

Joe showed them the place inside the barn where the Skadegamutc had assaulted Horus. A messy spot, with bits of dried blood on the floor from his damaged face. Chimalis held her hand over the dried blood to try to get a sense of what the creature looked like, how it behaved, how it moved. She had an inherent ability to see visions in her mind, but there was no Skadegamutc blood on the floor; only Horus's blood which, unfortunately, gave her little insight on the man.

"How is he doing?" Chimalis asked Joe.

"Horus? He's doing well. They performed surgery on his nose. He's still a little banged up, but he should be released from the hospital soon."

Joe nodded toward Chimalis. "Is your assistant, Luiz, going to attend the festival?"

Chimalis stood and brushed off her left pant leg. "Yes, he will. He's wrapping up the Pope Lick Creek incident in Kentucky. Should be here in a few days."

Niben looked up into the barn's ceiling, observing the multiple cracks in the wood. "Luiz was injured in Alaska, wasn't he?"

Chimalis nodded, unhappy with the question. "He was, and unfortunately, it was my fault."

Niben blanched. "Oh, I can't believe that. He was just doing his duty."

"A duty that I ordered him to do."

Niben walked over to Chimalis and laid her hand on her shoulder. "But, he's fine now, right?"

"Yes, thank the gods."

Niben smiled and followed Chimalis further into the barn. "Luiz is a good guy, isn't he?"

"He's the best agent I've ever had," Chimalis said, climbing up a ladder and reviewing the gaps in the ceiling. She took pictures of the gaps with her cell phone. Niben held on to the ladder while Chimalis conducted her investigation.

"Hey," Joe said, "I'm not a bad agent either."

Chimalis snickered. "Yes, but you're not my assistant. I'm yours."

Joe walked from one end of the barn to another, investigating areas where the Skadegamutc had skillfully avoided their attacks. Their wooden torches were on the ground, burned and covered in ash. "So," he said, looking up at Chimalis, "what do you think?"

Chimalis climbed down from the ladder, turned to Joe, and winked. "What I think is that, next time, you find a location where you can corner the bastard without massive gaps in the ceiling."

⌘

The second location was a home in which an entire family had been fed upon by the Skadegamutc. A Maliseet family which had, in the end, been destroyed.

Such a tragic event.

"They were brave," Joe said, guiding Chimalis through the house, showing her the areas where the creature had killed the victims. "They had publicly chastised the beast, and had reported his appearance at their house, when their ten-year-old daughter had died at the tip of its fangs."

Chimalis looked through the documents detailing their deaths. Pictures of their corpses were also shown, including the young girl whom Joe had mentioned. She wanted to tear up the pages and toss them aside. The images were overly graphic.

"Dreadful," Chimalis said, closing the dossier and handing it back to Joe. She whispered, "Reminds me of my fiancé's death."

Niben moved closer to Chimalis as she surveyed the physical damage the Skadegamutc had done to the home. Kitchen cabinets had been destroyed, including several mirrors in both their bedrooms and bathrooms. The front door had been demolished, and one of their beds had been torn to pieces.

"How did he die?" Niben asked.

Chimalis was reluctant to speak: the memories of his death were too painful, too prominent in her mind. But, it was often best to get it out, to tell the story and to confide in someone for comfort and support.

"We were working in South-Central Chile," she said, her eyes brimming with tears. "We were searching for Mapuche demons, which are often called *Wekufe*. They are soulless spirits that can disrupt and destroy the world's natural order. So, of course, we were worried about Chile. If those demons did their devil work in that country, then Chile might have fallen into chaos.

"So, my fiancé cornered the *Wekufe* in a cave and tried to vanquish them with my knife, but they cast terrible thoughts into his mind — regrets, failures, mistakes. He paused. I screamed at him to drive the knife into their throats, but he couldn't do it. He stood there, dropped the knife, and looked at me in sorrow. They then attacked him and… he was killed."

Niben turned Chimalis around and gave her a strong hug. "I'm so sorry, Chimalis. I wish there was something I could do to make you feel better."

"It's okay, sweetie," Chimalis said, hugging Niben back. She blinked away tears. "I wish I could have saved him. It was my duty to save him, and I failed to do so."

Joe sighed deeply and walked up to them. He was more than a little agitated. "I'm sorry, ladies, but can we keep our focus on the Skadegamutc?" He looked at Chimalis. "I'm very sorry for your loss, but we need to find this sorry son-of-a-bitch and kill it. We don't have a lot of time."

Chimalis pulled away from Niben. "Fine, fine," she said, brushing away the tears on her cheeks. She rolled her eyes. "As you wish, *Agent* Littlecloud. Let's head to the next location."

As they reached the car, Chimalis secretly pointed at Joe and whispered into Niben's ear, "The Skadegamutc might be an SOB, but *he's* the true son-of-a-bitch."

Niben chuckled quietly. "Oh, he's not so bad."

The third and final location was a mineshaft. It was where the Skadegamutc had previously resided. There were bones scattered about the floor of the shaft—some human, some animal—and claw marks along the wall as if people and animals had tried escaping. Cobwebs hung from the wooden braces supporting the mine. It was dark in the mine, but each person held a flashlight, waving it around to get a good look at all the dust and dirt.

"This was where he used to live," Joe said, kneeling beside a large hole in the floor. "He doesn't live here anymore, of course, and we don't know where he resides now. He had a coffin in this location, if you can believe it, like some hideous vampire in a movie. Horus and I trapped him here once, but unfortunately, he morphed into a ball of light and, again, slipped away."

Chimalis, studying the bones, shook her head. She held her hand over the dilapidated coffin, hoping to get a glimpse of where the creature might be living now. She closed her eyes and said a few silent prayers in Zuni. Nothing came to her.

"We have to figure out a way to prevent it from shifting into a ball of light," she said, disappointed that she couldn't divine its whereabouts. She stood and asked, "Is there any way we can keep it from doing so?"

"That's very difficult," Joe said. "There's really no way to prevent it from shifting. The key, I think, is to find it in human form and slam your knife into it, and burn it as well. A quick, immediate stab and set it aflame. That'll do the job."

Chimalis wasn't so sure. Yes, they could possibly corner it again, in some barn, house, or cave, and she could move quickly to vanquish its spirit. However, based on what had happened to Horus Ruth, Chimalis could be brutally injured.

Joe's cell phone activated. He moaned, took it out of his pocket, and walked toward the shaft entrance. "I'll be back in a minute."

Niben knelt beside the hole where the creature's coffin lay. She cast her flashlight on the scatter of bones. She picked up a femur and studied it. It was dark, soiled, and brittle. "Could you stab its ball of light?"

"What?"

"Could you *stab* it as a ball of light?"

*Why is she asking more questions about my knife?* "No, I don't think so. I've never done something like that before. Then again, no cryptid creature I know of has ever morphed into a ball of light. It doesn't usually work that way."

"Would the blade get damaged if you tried it?"

Chimalis stared at Niben, was about to come up with a lie to keep her from knowing too much about her knife, when Joe stepped back into the mine shaft. He stared at Chimalis, his face pure white.

"What's up?" Chimalis asked.

Joe put his phone away and said, his face grim, "We've got a serious problem in New Brunswick."

# CHAPTER SEVEN

*New Brunswick, Canada*

Technically, the FBI-VPA did not have jurisdiction in Canada, although it did have a strong relationship with Canadian police; more specifically, the Royal Canadian Mounted Police, or the so-called RCMP, the equivalent to the FBI. When Joe and Chimalis arrived in New Brunswick, the RCMP already had personnel at the location where the deadly attack by the Skadegamutc had taken place. Niben stayed behind in Maine. She had matters to attend to at the FBI office in Portland. Chimalis wondered what those "matters" were.

This was one of the most vicious attacks that Chimalis had ever seen: a casino hotel room in New Brunswick, with four bodies — two men, two women — strewn across the room like discarded balls of paper. The men had been tossed into the walls, their bodies broken, bloodied, and twisted. They had been drained of their blood and portions of their flesh had been eaten. The condition of the bodies of the two women was different. It seemed as if the creature had flown through them as a ball of light, burning their flesh straight through and cauterizing their wounds. Some of their flesh had been eaten as well.

The RCMP had lined up the bodies on the floor and were preparing to place them in body bags. Chimalis asked them to delay that action while she and Joe examined the bodies.

All four of the victims were in their twenties. Young, vibrant, deciding to come to the casino for fun and, hopefully, win some cash. Chimalis sighed as she studied the claw marks on the women's shoulders, and the deep penetration wound of the light ball.

"You know why the Skadegamutc came here, don't you?" Chimalis asked Joe.

"Why?"

"To divert our attention," Chimalis said. "To pull us away from Maine so that he can do whatever the hell he wants in that state."

Joe scoffed and shook his head. "He's been here before, Chimalis. In Canada. He's committed several crimes here. None as violent as this one, I'll grant you, but he's been here before: Quebec City, Montreal, Ottawa, and Toronto. The paperwork tells the story. This is standard practice for him."

"Nevertheless, I'm certain he's diverting our attention. Trust me, I know. I've seen cryptids do this before."

"Diverting our attention from what?"

"From..." Chimalis stood. She tugged on Joe's coat to guide him into a corner of the room so that they could speak privately.

"What?" Joe asked, with Chimalis following him into the corner. "What's the problem?"

Chimalis sighed, looked both ways, and whispered to keep the RCMP staff from hearing their conversation. "Look... how much do you trust Niben?"

"What the hell are you talking about?"

Chimalis put her hands on her waist and shook her head, staring into Joe's eyes. "I'm concerned about her."

"About what?"

Chimalis looked again at the RCMP and pulled Joe deeper into the corner. "She's been asking me a lot of question about my knife."

"So?" Joe shrugged and put up his hands. "She's part of our team now. You asked her to participate, remember? She needs to know how it functions to help you conduct the strike."

"She's asking too many questions: how is the knife used? What body part do I need to stab it with? How does it subsume spirits?" Chimalis shook her head. "Too much."

"Look," Joe sighed and smiled, "Niben is an effective VPA agent. She's given me guidance and assistance in the pursuit of this monster. I trust her completely."

"But, has she given you adequate information about the Skadegamutc?" Chimalis squinted. "You've been unsuccessful so far in defeating it. I wonder if her information is *inadequate*."

Joe pulled back. "Are you implying that she's deliberately giving me false information?"

Chimalis shook her head. "No. I'm simply wondering if maybe she doesn't have correct information about this creature. Perhaps she's just feeding you information to ingratiate herself to you. Perhaps she's not as good an agent as you believe her to be."

Joe's jaw muscles clenched and he balled his hands into fists. Chimalis moved her hand to the knife on her belt, prepared to defend herself if necessary should he shift into bear form.

Instead, he smiled. Relaxing his fists, he backed off another step. "Look, we need to focus on the murder of these people, okay? And, we need to take time to try to discover where the creature is, find him, and kill him. Will you help me with that, please?"

Chimalis stared into Joe's eyes and nodded. "Fine, but we need to do this quickly. We have the Wabanaki Festival coming up in a week. We need to get back to Maine soon. I've no doubt that the Skadegamutc is back in the state already."

Joe nodded, turned, and continued observing the bodies. Chimalis did the same, but in her mind, she could not stop thinking about Niben. She seemed like such a wonderful person. Sweet, kind, and she had allowed Chimalis to stay at her home.

*Maybe there's a reason for that*, Chimalis wondered as she looked at the deep, cauterized holes in the women's corpses. *Maybe Niben invited me to stay with her for an important reason.*

## In an Alley Near the FBI Office, Portland, Maine

The Skadegamutc drifted down, its ball of light illuminating the alley's brick walls. Niben stood there waiting for the creature to turn back into human form. She preferred it to be human-like, though its dark grey flesh and noxious smells were often too much for her to bear. It was difficult to speak directly to a ball of light: its voice was too loud, echoing off the walls, and potentially alerting other members of the FBI.

The creature had already been back in Maine for five days, and in that time, it had attacked campers at the Pine Ridge Campground: an elderly couple celebrating their wedding anniversary, and hikers walking along the Precipice Loop. As a VPA agent, Niben had "investigated" those areas, but she had declared them as apparent suicides, as per the Skadegamutc's orders.

The ball of light paused in front of her. Niben covered her eyes from the intense glow. Finally, it changed, the light shifting into human form. As the light dimmed, Niben lowered her hands and waited.

"Tell me," he said, his voice stronger now than it had been when he had drunk from Niben's arm in her home. "Tell me about Chimalis Burton."

She told him what she knew about Burton. First, she spoke of Chimalis' assistant, Luiz Vasquez, and their strong relationship, about how he had been severely injured in Alaska, and how Chimalis had blamed herself for the incident. She then spoke of Chimalis' fiancé, how he had been savaged by demons in Peru and how she, once again, blamed herself for his death. Finally, she spoke of the ceremonial knife, how it looked, how it functioned, and how Chimalis was planning on driving it into his flesh, and how his spirit and his soul would be vanquished. Niben provided as much detail as she could.

The Skadegamutc shivered. Niben couldn't tell if it was from fear or the elation of knowing so much about Chimalis. Perhaps both.

"Good," he said, moving closer to Niben. She could smell his foul breath and see his flesh dropping bits of dry grey skin from his arms. "Can you acquire her knife?"

She nodded. "Maybe. They are going to attend the Thoreau-Wabanaki Trail Festival in a few days, per my suggestion. I could try to steal it from her then."

He nodded. "Yes, you do that, and I will make ensure that Chimalis Burton never lives another day."

Niben's chest ached. Was she hyperventilating? A severe case of anxiety? She couldn't say, but one thing was certain: "Joe Littlecloud would be the better person to kill."

"What?"

"He is the one that has tried to kill you multiple times. It's best to try to end *his* life. Trying to kill Chimalis would be a difficult task, maybe impossible. She's a good person."

The Skadegamutc stared at Niben, his eyes glowing brightly, his face turning deep black. Niben cowered before him, feeling his intimidation. "She will use that knife of hers to kill *me*. You understand that, don't you?"

Niben nodded. "Yes."

"And so, while she is there at the festival, you will take the knife from her while I make her feel worthless, despondent. She will die at the festival, and in time, I *will* take care of Joe Littlecloud as well. Understand?"

Niben lowered her head as if in prayer. "Yes. I will do as you say."

"Good. Now go. Do your duty and get me her knife."

The Skadegamutc backed off into shadow, turned, and shifted back into a ball of light. Niben watched as the ball slid up over the building and disappeared.

She had been ordered to take the knife. She could do that, for sure. But, to see Chimalis die. No, that was not going to happen. She knew what the monster was going to do to the woman, and Niben would do everything she could to keep it from happening. *Chimalis is a good person, a good agent. I cannot let her die.*

Niben turned, walked out of the alley, and back into the FBI office.

# Chapter Eight

At the Thoreau-Wabanaki Trail Festival, Moosehead Lake

Chimalis was delighted by the festivities around her. She and Joe were there, eating traditional Wabanaki food, while appreciating Maine's cultural heritage and natural resources. Another aspect of the festival was the Naturalist Henry David Thoreau, who apparently had taken three trips into the woodlands of Maine. He was an essayist, a poet, and a philosopher. He was best known for his book Walden. Chimalis had never read it, although she had read his essay "Civil Disobedience," a wonderful treatise about citizens rising up against unjust laws.

Another part of the festival revolved around hikes into Maine woodlands, canoe rides on Moosehead Lake and some of the surrounding rivers. Both Chimalis and Joe opted out of those trips, as their focus at the festival was to try to interview the Wabanaki people about the Skadegamutc and to try to figure out where the creature resided.

It was late at night, nearly ten o'clock, and Joe and Chimalis sat near a bonfire, listening to the origin story of the Wabanaki people. According to the legend, a Wabanaki hero, *Gluskabe*, often pronounced as *Glooscap*, came to earth and created all the animals. He then shot arrows into multiple white Ash trees and thus, created the tribes of the Wabanaki federation. Chimalis watched in awe as Maliseet dancers played out the story in rhythmic motions. Joe, sitting next to her, seemed bored and impatient.

The ceremony concluded an hour later. Joe and Chimalis then met with the Mi'kmaq tribal leader, Pasmay Gould. The man wore a coat of woolen cloth, adorned with silk ribbon appliques. He also wore green glass beads around his neck and a black hat with traditional Mi'kmaq designs wrapped around the band.

"What can I do for you, Joe Littlecloud?" Pasmay asked, guiding them into his wigwam. "Please, sit. Let us talk."

Inside the tent, tree boughs covered the floor, along with blankets made of animal hide. The walls bore paintings of nature and animals. Chimalis looked at all of them, hoping to see if any cryptids had been drawn. Fortunately, none had been. It was clear to her that neither the Mi'kmaq, nor any of the other tribes of the wigwam, were interested in drawing evil creatures that would cause harm to the Wabanaki. In the center of the wigwam lay a small fire pit. Pasmay Gould sat on the opposite side of the fire.

Joe and Chimalis sat beside each other on a bear quilt covering the ground. They crossed their legs and waited. Pasmay Gould took a long drag from a wooden pipe. Chimalis couldn't tell if it was an actual peace pipe. Perhaps it was, but it possessed no symbols or images suggesting peace or unity. Pasmay handed the pipe to Joe. He took a long drag. He then handed it to Chimalis, who was not in favor of smoking, but tradition demanded that she, at least, give it one puff. She put the pipe in her mouth and drew smoke. She exhaled quickly to ensure that she didn't cough her lungs out. She then handed it back to the tribal leader.

Pasmay accepted the pipe gracefully, took another drag, blew smoke from his mouth, and said, "So what can I do for you, Joe Littlecloud?"

"You can tell me where the Skadegamutc resides."

The tribal leader paused, lowered his pipe, and nodded. "I am aware of that vile beast, and I am glad that you pursue it for its elimination," he said, "but I'm sad to say that I've no knowledge of its whereabouts."

Joe shook his head. "Are you sure? Agent Niben Bellerose of the VPA informed me that you knew exactly where it was." He raised his arms and moved his hands around the room. "Is he somewhere nearby? Far away? Tell me what you know."

Pasmay shook his head and laid his pipe on the deer hide on which he was sitting. "I am sorry, Joe, but I do not know where it lives. It has assaulted the Mi'kmaq people on occasion—a sad, sad tragedy, indeed—but I do not know where it resides."

Joe rubbed his face, clearly agitated. By what, Chimalis wondered? By the truth that Pasmay did not know where the creature lived or that Niben had, perhaps, given falsehoods about the Mi'kmaq leader's knowledge? And, where was Niben? Chimalis, again, wondered. She was supposed to be here at the festival. Chimalis had seen her early on, when the festivities began. They had sat together to watch a few ceremonial dances, and then, she had vanished.

Joe pointed a finger at Pasmay. "In the '90s, your people suffered tremendously from that beast. You yourself even confronted him once."

Pasmay nodded. "Yes, and in the mine shaft that you drove him out of. I remember. I did try to locate him and destroy him, but I failed. He was too strong. He nearly broke my jaw." He picked up his pipe and puffed. Again, he blew smoke from his mouth and let it drift up and out of the wigwam. "He then shifted into a ball of light and disappeared. Since then, I have not been able to find him."

Joe climbed onto his knees and barked at Pasmay. "You know where he is, dammit! Tell me… tell me now, or I will accuse you of telling lies and—"

"Okay," Chimalis roared, "that's enough!" Chimalis stood and pointed to the exit. "Joe… outside. Now!"

Chimalis exited the wigwam. A minute later, Joe stepped outside, his face a deep red. She put her hands on her waist and said, "Why were you being such an *ass* to that man? Why accuse him of lying?"

Joe turned and looked back into the wigwam, staring intently at Pasmay, who continued to smoke his pipe beyond the flames of the fire pit. "That son of a bitch knows where the Skadegamutc is. Niben said so."

Chimalis shrugged. "Maybe Niben didn't give you correct information."

Joe stepped away, trying to calm himself. "No. She knows Pasmay; they've been friends for years, and she knows that *he* knows where it is. He's trying to protect it. I just know it."

*Not a wise choice, Joe,* Chimalis thought, but kept the thought to herself. Hadn't she already discussed Niben's questionable information with Joe in Canada? Yet, Joe didn't seem to accept her doubts. Chimalis didn't know why. Were he and Niben *that* close? Were they in a physical relationship? She did not know, but one thing was certain: throughout her time as a VPA agent, Niben had not provided Joe with adequate information about the Skadegamutc.

Chimalis wondered: *is Niben in cahoots with this creature?* The thought of it terrified her.

She shook her head, sighed, and said, "Look... why don't you go and find Niben. She's supposed to be here. Maybe she just gave you the wrong information by mistake." Chimalis put her hand on Joe's shoulder. "Go find her and try to get more information."

Joe nodded and tried to smile. "Okay, I'll do so. Are you coming with me?"

"No," Chimalis said, looking up at the night sky. "I need to take a walk and get some fresh air."

Chimalis needed more than fresh air. She needed to mingle among the patrons, to learn the Wabanaki culture, to meet and greet as many tribesmen as she could. She shook hands, watching ceremonies and discussing Wabanaki cultural traits and traditions. While she wandered and mingled, she avoided the forest edge where the Skadegamutc might well lurk as a ball of light, floating in the canopy, watching her as she enjoyed the festivities and the fresh air.

She walked through the vast field of parked cars. Some people were already leaving the festival; others continued to celebrate their heritage. She heard the crowd and saw the various bonfires among the gathered. She smiled. She liked the festivities a lot.

She decided to step closer to Moosehead Lake. As the events in Alaska had proven, she still wasn't too keen on water, lakes and rivers, but she had grown less anxious. Her adventures underneath Kenai Lake while fighting the Qalupalik had given her strength and confidence. She was not as afraid of water anymore.

Chimalis stepped up to the edge of the lake. She looked again into the clear sky. Bright stars glimmered in the darkness, and the moon was as bright as she had seen it in a long, long time. Again, she smiled and basked in the strong glow of the moon. It felt refreshing.

*It's your fault!*

A voice, small, speaking indistinct words, echoed through her mind.

*Your fault! You killed them. You killed them all.*

The images of all the FBI agents who had drowned in Kenai Lake struck Chimalis's mind like a hammer, each of their faces clear in her memory, each of them falling below the surface, opening their mouths, sucking in the cold, dirty water, and drowning.

She dropped to her knees, shivering, her heart beating rapidly. Their faces remained in her mind, turning white, icy, as if their skin would shatter in the lake and leave nothing but bones and brittle teeth.

*You killed us*, they said together, pointing their clammy fingers at her, condemning her with brutal words. *You killed us. Our families mourn our deaths.*

And, it was true... so true. She had ordered those agents and her partner, Luiz, to Quartz Creek to try to find, trap, and kill the Qalupalik. A bad, bad decision. And now she was technically on "administrative leave" so that the FBI could determine if she was at fault for their deaths. *Of course I am,* Chimalis thought, not being able to erase from her mind the terrible murders of those agents. *I killed them all.*

She turned back to Moosehead Lake and crawled slowly into the waves sloshing against the shore. The moon's pull was strong tonight, raising the tide of the lake as if it were the Atlantic Ocean. Chimalis paused and tried to stop crawling further into the water. Her hands and feet were under the waves.

*I love you, Chimalis.*

She saw now the face of her fiancé, smiling, his eyes aglow. He stood in the cave in Chile with the Mapuche demons closing in. She reached out toward the lake, the smiling face of her fiancé mere inches away. She reached for him, tried to grab his collar and pull him back, pull him to safety.

The demons attacked. They bit his legs, his arms, tearing his flesh from his body like paper. He screamed as blood spattered everywhere. Chimalis reached out again for his face, but one of the demons bit his cheek and shredded it straight down to his neck. Her fiancé reached for her; she reached for him. His smile disappeared, replaced by a scowl as his face peeled away until the bones of his skull shown like a bright white beacon in the night. The demons chewed on his eyes.

*It's your fault, Chimalis,* the shattered face of her fiancé said. *All your fault. You gave me your knife, but I wasn't prepared to use it. Your fault. All your fault.*

She burst into tears. dread blossomed in her chest such as she had never felt before, her mind full of sorrow and anguish. *I cannot live,* she thought as she continued crawling through the lake. *I've killed so many people. I cannot go on.*

Chimalis crawled further into the lake, her arms and legs now covered in dark, dirty water, her hands and feet sinking into the soft mud. She tried resisting again, but the images and accusations, the guilt, the destroyed face of her fiancé, were too strong. She even felt guilt for her parents' passing, as if she had been responsible for their deaths as well.

Chimalis spread her arms wide as if she were praising the Wabanaki. She paused, looked up into the bright moon, and saw a flickering ball of light pass across it. She then closed her eyes and dropped.

She fell face down into the water and lay there, waiting to die.

Chimalis floated in the lake, her arms out, her mouth open. She felt free, liberated. It felt *right* that she would die because she had killed so many people in her past, so many cryptids as well. It was time to say goodbye to everything.

She dropped lower. She sucked in the dirty water. Her lungs ached. She twitched but resisted the pain in her chest. *It is done,* she said, a weak smile curling her lips. *It is done...*

From above the surface, hands grabbed her and pulled her up and out of the lake.

She tried resisting, but the strength of the person gripping her collar was too great. Chimalis opened her eyes, gagged, and spit out the water in her lungs. She coughed violently as her rescuer pulled her to shore, laid her down, and pressed her chest.

The person's mouth covered hers. Soft lips, tender lips. She breathed air into her lungs and continued pressing her chest. Again, and again.

Chimalis's eyes opened. She coughed, leaned over, and spit more water out on the ground.

Her rescuer spoke softly. "You're safe now, Chimalis." A woman's voice, faint, confident, and familiar. "Stay alive, my friend. Stay alive and fight that bastard like a Zuni warrior."

Chimalis opened her eyes again and tried to see who the person was, but she was gone. Chimalis turned and lay on her back, breathing heavily.

Joe Littlecloud and others still at the festival came to her aid.

He knelt and lifted her carefully. Her legs were weak, but he held her firmly. "What happened, Chimalis? Are you all right?"

He seemed concerned, nearly afraid by his expression. Chimalis looked at him, took in his wide and fearful eyes. She nodded, turned her head, and spit out more water. "I'm okay. I'm..."

She reached for her belt and her knife. The sheath was open. The blade was gone.

She stood quickly despite her weak legs; her mind still dizzy with painful images and fear. She reached for her knife again. She pushed Joe away and looked everywhere, on the ground, in the water, in the sky.

"My knife!" Chimalis shouted. *"Where's my knife?"*

# Chapter Nine

*Midnight, Ten Miles from Moosehead Lake*

Niben pulled into a gravel road leading to an abandoned cabin. A cabin where, years ago, the Skadegamutc had murdered an innocent family on vacation. They too had attended the Thoreau-Wabanaki Trail festival, and then they were found the next morning by the FBI as nothing but dried husks. Her stomach churned. She had no desire to step out of her car and show the beast what she had taken from Chimalis, but she had no choice. If she didn't do as he directed, she'd be dead.

She turned off the ignition, climbed out of her car, and waited in the dark. It was quiet, deathly quiet, to the point of terrifying. *Perhaps he isn't here*, she thought. *Perhaps he's somewhere else, killing more innocent people.* The thought angered and terrified her in equal measure. But, she waited, and waited, and waited, until a large ball of light appeared, hovering in the thick canopy of trees over the old, boarded-up cabin. A light breeze rustled the leaves in the trees while the ball dropped to the ground. The light shimmered then shifted as the Skadegamutc, in human form, walked out of the forest toward Niben.

"You have failed me, Niben," he said, his face dark again. "You failed me."

Niben pulled the knife from her belt. "No, I did not." She lifted the knife above her head. "Look... see? I got the knife."

The Skadegamutc drew closer. She could only see him in shadow, her car headlights casting light into the ruined cabin. "I wanted her *dead*, but you saved her. Why?"

His grey skin seemed to ooze blood. His sharp fangs drew closer to her neck. Niben ignored his question, shivered in place, but tried to remain calm. "Take the knife. You can use it to kill Joe."

The Skadegamutc pulled the knife from her hand. He studied it, turned it over and over to see the flash of cryptid icons along the pulsing blade. He nodded. "It is a fine blade, and it is good that you've acquired it. But, you saved Chimalis from dying. She would have drowned in Moosehead Lake, but you saved her. I ask again: why?"

"Because... I like her. I respect her. She doesn't deserve to die. Joe is the one who should be killed."

The Skadegamutc slapped Niben hard. The power of the blow tossed her against the car. The glass on the driver's side door shattered. Niben slid to the ground and howled in pain.

"You betrayed me, Niben!"

Niben groaned and clutched her shoulders. "I betrayed no one, you sorry son-of-a-bitch!"

"Chimalis should have died." He reached her, pulled her up by the throat, and tossed her toward the cabin. Niben struck the ground and rolled into thick grass. "With Chimalis still alive, she becomes a threat to me. Joe is nothing. Joe is... insignificant. I tried to kill her. I filled her with pain and sorrow. She wanted to drown herself, but you saved her. She is a danger to me, Niben, and now you are as well."

Niben, her left shoulder dislocated, her face covered in blood and bruises, her uniform torn and muddy, reached for her pistol. She pulled it from her belt and aimed it at the Skadegamutc.

The creature grabbed her wrist and pointed the gun upward. Niben fired three shots into the sky, echoing through the forest.

The sudden vibration of the shots loosened the Skadegamutc's grip. Niben's arm dropped, and she fired another round. It tore through the beast's shoulder. He howled and fell back. She tried pulling the trigger again to put a bullet through his chest, but the Skadegamutc slammed his fist into the pistol and knocked it out of Niben's hand.

He launched himself at her, screaming, "By my virtue, you shall die!" He sunk his fangs into her throat. Niben tried pushing him away, but her dislocated shoulder ached. She didn't have enough strength to fight him off.

He sank his fangs deeper into her throat, and her precious blood spread down her uniform. She tried kicking him, tried beating his face and shoulders, but her heartbeat was too fast. She could not stop the blood draining from her neck. She tried again to push him away, but her strength succumbed to his feeding.

She felt nauseated, felt her life draining from her neck. She closed her eyes. *I am going to die,* she thought, her strength fading away, *but so long as Chimalis lives and kills this bastard, I'll be content. I am Penobscot. I am* Panawáhpskewi, *the People of Where the White Rocks Extend Out. I am going to die, but I am at peace.*

# Chapter Ten

"Are you okay, boss?"

Her partner, Luiz Vasquez, had finally joined the investigation. After his stint with the Pope Lick Creek monster in Kentucky, he was more than willing to arrive in Maine and assist in any way he could. Luiz was a good agent; again, one of the best that Chimalis had ever worked with.

She turned to him and blinked. "What?"

"Are you okay?" Luiz asked again. "You look a little... pale."

And rightfully so, for in the trees above them hung Niben Bellerose, arms down, hair wet and knotted, a puddle of dried blood on the ground below her. A chunk of flesh had been torn out of her neck. She was stiff with rigor mortis. FBI agents were trying to cut her down.

"She saved my life, Luiz," Chimalis said. "She dragged me out of the lake, resuscitated me." Chimalis suddenly looked dour. "But she took my knife."

Ten minutes later, the agents carefully brought Niben down and laid her on the ground. Chimalis and Joe put on their blue nitrile gloves and checked the body.

It was clear that she had been brutalized by the Skadegamutc. There was no other explanation. Her car's window had been shattered, and there were dents along the doors where the beast had obviously thrown her. Chimalis checked Niben's neck. It revealed clear signs of teeth marks, and all her blood had been extracted. There was only one explanation for why she had been killed.

*She saved my life,* Chimalis thought as Joe observed the body and discovered some broken bones in Niben's chest. *She saved my life, and the Skadegamutc killed her for it.*

Chimalis was in tears. So was Joe. He hadn't said much since Niben's body had been discovered. He was trying to maintain his composure, whispering to the FBI agents nearby, detailing Niben's condition. "Broken bones in her chest. Two loose teeth. Bruises on her face. A severe tear in her neck along the carotid artery, possibly a self-inflicted wound. Possible suicide—"

"Oh, come on, Joe!" Chimalis said, annoyed by his inability to accept the obvious truth. "You know exactly what happened here. Niben was killed by the Skadegamutc. Suicide? *Really?* Are you nuts?"

"Watch yourself, Chimalis," Joe said, his expression just as dour as hers. "I'm not going to tolerate your accusations against Niben. This could very well have been a suicide."

Chimalis sighed deeply and pointed to the tree from which Niben had hung. "Explain to me how a suicide victim could have hung herself from the tree. Explain it to me."

Joe shrugged. "It's not an atypical situation, Chimalis. Suicide victims often hang themselves from trees."

"Yeah, with a noose around their neck, but that's not what Niben did." Chimalis turned Niben's arm over to reveal scars along the forearm. "Dammit, man, isn't it obvious? Look at her arm. Scars all over her skin. These are teeth marks, Joe. She's been enthralled to the Skadegamutc for years, and she's been feeding you lies for a long time."

It was clear that Joe wasn't going to believe the truth. Niben had been a confidant to him for so long and he just couldn't accept that his friend had been enthralled to this beast for, as Chimalis said, years.

"Look," Chimalis said, working around Niben's waist, touching her belt and working her hands on the small of her back. She pulled her hands out and opened them. "See? No knife. Niben stole my knife, and guess who she gave it to?"

"Really?" Luiz said, surprised. "What are you going to do now that—"

"I cannot stay here without my knife," Chimalis interrupted. A tear ran down her face. "I—I have to go."

"What the hell are you talking about?" Joe stood, his expression beyond shock. "You're leaving the investigation?"

"I cannot vanquish the Skadegamutc without my knife." Chimalis stood. She stepped over Niben and approached Joe. "The knife is what matters. I'm sorry, Joe, but I cannot help you anymore."

Joe deflated and scowled at her. "You *coward*. Chimalis Burton... the supposed finest VPA agent in the world. But you clearly don't have the courage to keep going." He shook his head. "I'm disappointed in you, Bluebird. I thought you had more courage than that."

Chimalis clenched her teeth. She poked Joe's chest with a stiff finger. "And you've been a fool for years, chasing this beast while relying on a woman who lied to you all the time. You're as naive as a child, Joe. Some great *di-yin* shaman you are! I understand now why that Mescalero cursed you."

Joe grabbed Chimalis's collar. He pulled her closer. "Now, you listen to me—"

Luiz grabbed Joe's arms and pushed them apart. "That's enough! You two back off, now. Joe... let her go!"

Joe released her collar and backed away. He waved Chimalis off. "Fine. You want to leave, then get out of here. I don't need your knife or your help. I'll kill the beast on my own. I don't need you anymore."

Chimalis, with tears running down her face, pushed Luiz aside and walked toward his rental car. Luiz followed.

"Boss," he asked, "what about your knife?"

"It's gone," she blurted.

"Yes, but if the Skadegamutc has it, shouldn't you go aft—"

"It's gone! I'm not going after that beast!" She opened the passenger door on Luiz's rental and climbed in. She slammed the door shut. "Take me to the airport, Luiz. I'm not staying here any longer."

# CHAPTER ELEVEN

*Three Weeks Later, Near Portland, Maine*

Joe remembered an old Apache saying: *It is better to have less thunder in the mouth and more lightning in the hand.* He wished that he had lightning in the hand, like the emperor in the old *Star Wars* movies. If so, he'd burn the beast to cinders, and what a joy that would be!

According to VPA reports, the Skadegamutc had been seen near Willard Beach. Thus, Joe was carefully tracking the beast near a long line of rental houses. It was late in the afternoon and the sun was setting in the west. He had a small can of gasoline and a lighter. The creature's footprints were prominent along the sand, though they zigged and zagged, Joe supposed, to keep him confused and out of step. But, Joe was no fool. He was an Apache shaman, and he knew how to follow tracks.

VPA reports indicated that the Skadegamutc was possibly in one of the rental houses along Willard Beach. Feeding on innocent victims, no doubt, though some of the houses were empty. Joe moved swiftly toward the row of houses. Some had their lights on, some did not. He chose the ones without lights. Made sense, since the Skadegamutc typically did its devil work in the dark.

There were five houses in total alongside the beach. Joe investigated the two without lights. He moved toward the first one. He peeked into the windows. Nothing but darkness and luckily, no voices, no sounds. He then canvassed the second house. It was different. Though there were no discernable sounds, he did catch a glimpse of a shadow moving along the walls inside the house. Joe suddenly felt a twinge of guilt in his gut, his anxiety increasing. He moved up the porch to the front door and looked inside.

The Skadegamutc was there, behind the door, staring at him through the glass. Joe could smell him.

The door burst open, shattering into multiple pieces. Joe fell backward onto the porch, still holding his gasoline can and lighter. He pushed away splintered wood and tried to stand, flicking the lighter open. The Skadegamutc howled, put out his hand, and Joe's mind swirled with pain, sorrow, and bad memories.

The first time that he had gotten drunk and puked all over his dormitory floor. The first time that he had slapped his girlfriend and blamed it on her. The first time that he had married in his twenties. Their first child who had died from SIDS three weeks later. His inexplicable feeling of loss and shame. His continual drinking and physical abuse of his wife. Screaming at her. Slapping her. Kicking her in the stomach, and her reporting his abuse to that Mescalero shaman. A curse placed upon him so that he would never forget his constant drinking and aggressive behavior. His pleading for forgiveness and yet, his Apache community refusing to release him from the curse. So much pain, so much incalculable guilt. He felt like dying.

The Skadegamutc stood above him, licking its dark grey lips. "Feel your pain," it said. "Absorb it and know that you are going to die."

*I can't let this happen*, Joe thought as he tried pushing the horrific memories out of his mind. *I've no other choice.*

Joe screamed at the Skadegamutc and kicked its leg. Then, he changed, shifting his body into bear form, his clothes ripping across his thick, brown fur. He shouted again, his roar loud and distinct as his face elongated, his muzzle growing thick, his body spreading out broadly, his teeth sharp and powerful. He rose up on his hind legs, roared in bear form, and knocked the Skadegamutc back into the dark, empty house.

The Skadegamutc slammed into the couch, shrieked in pain, collected itself, and stood upright. It pulled out a knife, and despite Joe morphing in bear form, he recognized the blade.

Chimalis's knife, pulsing with blue light, seemingly eager to tear away Joe's flesh and subsume his spirit. Joe bounded into the living room, howled again, and attacked the beast.

The Skadegamutc tried thrusting the knife into the bear's massive throat, but the blade was knocked out of its hand. Joe slammed into the beast and tried to claw through its chest, but the Skadegamutc was more powerful than he realized. Joe tried to sink his fangs into the creature's throat, but he was knocked back as claws tore away at his muzzle in tight, precise cuts.

The Skadegamutc reached for the knife again, and Joe bit its arm, tearing away its grey flesh. It was clear now that the creature was trying to shift into a ball of light, but Joe continued to tear away at its arms, face, and throat. The Skadegamutc moved swiftly, blocking most of the attacks, though some blows found their mark. Joe was confident now that it was just a matter of time before he finally, at long last, destroyed this beast and put an end to its deadly reign.

The two scuffled back and forth, reaching out and tearing at each other's skin. Joe's brown fur was thick, but the Skadegamutc was able to work his hands underneath his coat and draw blood. The Skadegamutc kept trying to shift into light, but it seemed too weak and too terrified at Joe's massive bear body. *This is it*, he thought, preparing to shift back into human form and collect the gasoline and lighter. *I have him. I finally have him.*

Joe tried to shift, and an image appeared in his mind. The one of his little daughter, lying there in her crib, not breathing, lifeless, a victim of SIDS. She was so sweet, so beautiful. He could not keep himself from seeing his child, her sweet hair, her soft skin, her gentle face. In his mind, he reached out for her, and the Skadegamutc attacked.

It grabbed the knife as Joe peered, through illusion, into his daughter's crib. It turned the blade toward Joe Littlecloud and stabbed him.

He felt a warm sensation, a trickle of blood down his back. Blue energy coursed through his body as his bear form began to fade. He felt weak and confused. He reached for the knife to pull it out, but it was too close to the center of his spine. He fell to the floor.

*I'm going to die*, Joe said, feeling his soul rush out of his body and encircle the blade. *Like Niben did, like my child did.* He turned his head, now in human form, and stared at the Skadegamutc. The beast stared back at him, smiling, but saying nothing. It just watched as Joe's soul encircled the blade while his eyes slowly, slowly, closed forever.

# CHAPTER TWELVE

*Aspen, Colorado*

Chimalis sat on her couch, drinking coffee and staring out the window. This time of year, Aspen was marvelous. The high mountain peaks had snow, despite the warm weather below. The sun was setting; lights were flashing among all the homes along the valley. She couldn't hear anything, neither voices nor vehicles. Her house was quiet and still, save for the refrigerator occasionally making popping noises and the warm breeze rustling the trees outside her window. She drank her coffee and closed her eyes.

She couldn't stop thinking about the stress and sorrow that she had felt at the Thoreau-Wabanaki Trail festival. Her feelings were so strong and agonizing there that she had tried drowning herself. She remembered that the El Cadejo could put horrible thoughts into a person's mind, and so too the Qalupalik. Why, then, was she so determined to engage and vanquish these kinds of creatures? Why go through all the psychological trauma that could drive someone to the brink of death? The Skadegamutc's ability to conjure hurtful images in the mind was even stronger than El Cadejo or the Qalupalik. Physically, it was not as strong as the Atasaya that she had vanquished here in Colorado, but the Skadegamutc was, as Joe had called it, a 'beast'.

*Maybe I should resign.*

It made sense: why continually go through all the mental anguish that she had experienced these many years? The pain would, inevitably, lead her to drinking or taking pills to help drive away the blues. She wasn't much of a drinker, nor had she ever taken drugs. *And I won't*, she thought. *Never, never, never.*

But, what to do? Chimalis sipped her coffee and tried figuring it out. Resign from the VPA… and then what? What would she do then? Work at a grocery store? In a bookstore? A library? Work at one of Aspen's resorts and teach people how to ski? Chimalis couldn't help but chuckle at these notions. And yet, her ceremonial knife was gone. What could she possibly do to benefit the VPA without her knife? And why hadn't she stayed with Joe Littlecloud to pursue the Skadegamutc and recover her knife? She knew why: that creature was too powerful, both mentally and physically. It had terrorized and abused Niben as well, forcing her to do its bidding, forcing her to lie about its location and actions to Joe. Niben was dead now. A foolish thing for the Skadegamutc to do. Now, it had no support in the VPA and perhaps never would again. Could it move to another state and try to enthrall another VPA agent? Maybe, but unlikely. The Skadegamutc lived in Maine, and there, it would remain.

Her cell phone rang. Chimalis picked it up, saw the name on the screen, and swiped right.

"Luiz," she said. Luiz had chosen to stay in Maine to help Joe find the Skadegamutc, but not in a physical capacity. At the airport, Chimalis made sure that Luiz promised that he would stay in the office and help monitor the creature's whereabouts via civilian reports and video tracking. "How goes it?"

Luiz paused and breathed a strong sigh over the phone. Then he said, "Joe is dead, boss."

Anxiety gripped her chest. She felt dizzy. "How?"

"The Skadegamutc got him. Killed him in a house on Willard Beach."

Chimalis felt like crying, but no. Not this time. If she blamed herself for his death, like she had blamed herself repeatedly for other deaths, the Skadegamutc would see that pain and throw it back at her. She was saddened by Joe's death, for sure, but she couldn't blame herself. Not this time.

"How did he die?" she asked.

Luiz paused, then, "He was stabbed by your knife, boss. The blade vanquished him. He had shifted into bear form and, apparently, fought the creature hard. By all accounts, he was doing well and had caused some serious damage to the creature. FBI even found traces of its blood and skin fragments on the floor. Then the Skadegamutc stabbed him and subsumed his spirit."

A true sadness. "Was the knife recovered?" she asked.

"Yes. The Portland FBI recovered it. They have it here in the office."

All of Chimalis's anxiety suddenly faded away. What a relief! "Very well," she said. "I'll fly back to Portland and get the knife, and then we'll—"

"The blade is cracked, boss," Luiz said, and Chimalis could tell that he too was on the verge of tears. "I don't think it can be used again."

# CHAPTER THIRTEEN

Chimalis held the knife in her hand, studying the crack running from the tip of the blade to the base. She ran her finger along the damage. Blue light shimmered inside the blade, and she knew now that it was useless. Joe Littlecloud's bear form had been so large that it had overwhelmed the knife and caused it to fracture. Chimalis pulled the blade closer to her eyes and saw Joe's bear icon, severed in two by the crack. All the images of the cryptids that she had vanquished with her knife were still on the blade. That, at least, was a blessing, for none of their spirits had escaped. All of their souls were still inside. *Thank the gods*, she thought, carefully putting the knife back in its sheath, attached to her belt.

She would have to take it back to New Mexico and get Zuni spiritualists to repair the blade. Otherwise, the blue energy pulsing inside would grow more intense, and eventually, all the cryptids would escape. And that, Chimalis knew, could not occur. To allow that to happen would mean more deaths in the United States, and even more Native American deaths. She'd have to take the blade back soon.

But, not yet, not now. Now, she and Luiz were in the conference room that she, Joe, and Niben had been in at the beginning of the investigation. They were trying to figure out their next course of action.

"What now, boss?" Luiz asked. They were sitting at the table across from each other. "The VPA did recover some blood from the Skadegamutc and, as I said, bit traces of its skin. They also found DNA traces, within the creature's blood, from the four victims in New Brunswick. The fact that they found those traces suggests that—"

"It suggests that Joe did his job," Chimalis said, rubbing her hands together to make them warm and to keep them from shaking. "Joe damaged that bastard, badly, and now it's probably lying low to heal. Question is, where?"

Luiz shrugged. "It could have gone back to New Brunswick."

Chimalis shook her head. "Unlikely. That would require a lot of energy from the beast, and I suspect it's been weakened."

"Then it's here," Luiz said, nodding. "In Maine."

Chimalis agreed. "But where do we start?"

It could take days, weeks, or even months to track it down, and Chimalis did not have that kind of time. She had to deliver the knife to the spiritualists within a couple weeks or face serious consequences.

She sighed and rubbed her face. She leaned back in the chair and laid her head on the headrest. Closing her eyes, she tried to imagine where the creature had gone. It certainly wasn't near Portland right now. It had killed Joe Littlecloud near Willard Beach, which was indeed near Portland, but it wouldn't possibly stay here. The VPA would be all over it if it had. It could have travelled back to Moosehead Lake. That's where it had killed Niben. It could very well be back in that cave that she and Joe and Niben had investigated. *Yeah*, she thought, *if it was stupid*. The VPA would be all over those locations as well, and if it were in one of them, it would be found. No. It was somewhere else, somewhere comfortable, resting and healing.

"How are we going to find it, boss?" Luiz asked.

Chimalis opened her eyes and leaned forward in her chair. "The only way I can think of is through dream trance." She nodded. "I'll have to contact Halian."

Halian had helped her locate and vanquish El Cadejo. He was in his seventies and a Zuni Priest of the Bow. He and her mother had grown up together.

"Okay," Luiz said, "but how do we kill it once we find it?" He paused, seemingly embarrassed. "You don't have your knife anymore."

"I know how to kill it."

Chimalis turned and saw a man standing at the entrance of the conference room. His face had bruises, and he wore a clear plastic mask on his face. The plastic mask made him look almost synthetic, like some robot or creepy artificial intelligence.

"Are you... Horus Ruth?" Chimalis asked.

The man nodded. "Yes. And I know exactly how to kill it."

She stood and walked over to the man. He still had swelling underneath the plastic mask. She approached and squinted. "How?"

Horus raised a match and flicked the tip. It ignited quickly, the smell of sulfur growing. He smiled. "With fire."

"Why in hell didn't Joe tell me about this?" Chimalis was quite frustrated.

"Because I think he knew that your knife would vanquish the beast." Horus sat down at the table. "He wanted you to kill it and subsume its spirit so that it would be locked in your blade forever. Unfortunately, he's dead now."

Chimalis could see that Horus was beside himself with grief, though she couldn't understand why he had returned to the FBI. He was Joe's assistant, not an "official" VPA agent. He could have simply walked away. *He wants to avenge Joe's death*, she thought. Made sense. They had been good friends for ages.

"My blade is damaged." Chimalis pulled the knife from her sheath and showed it to Horus. "It can't be used against the Skadegamutc." She took the knife back and tucked it away. "So, how do we burn it?"

Horus shrugged. "We find it, corner it, keep it from shifting into a ball of light, and then douse it with gasoline. Then, we light the fire. We watch it burn down to ashes, and then we scoop it up and spread it into the wind."

"Do you know where it is, Horus?" Luiz asked.

"No, but based on the injuries that Joe delivered, I wouldn't think it'd be very far."

"Maybe, maybe not." Chimalis stood, and it was clear to her exactly what she had to do. "To find this monster, I'll have to go into trance."

"A trance?" Horus turned and looked at her. "Where?"

Where, indeed? Chimalis paused and looked out the door. Other FBI agents were doing their duty: deskwork, making calls, and heading out for various investigations. Too bad that the VPA in Maine was so small. Without Joe and Niben, there were now only three agents to head the investigation against the Skadegamutc: Chimalis, Luiz, and Horus. And where in *hell* would they find that bloody beast?

Chimalis turned and looked at Horus. "I need to go to the cemetery where Lucas Maske's body was buried. Do you know where it is?"

Horus turned, looked at Luiz, then turned back. He rolled his eyes and nodded, the plastic mask shifting slightly on his face. "Yes, I know where he's buried."

# CHAPTER FOURTEEN

*Millinocket Town Cemetery*

Chimalis knelt on a quilt beside Lucas Maske's gravesite. It was nearly midnight with a clear sky. She wore a light jacket, for the breeze blowing down from Canada was unseasonably cool. She placed two candles in front of the man's tombstone so that the wind would not blow them out and so that she could see his name and epitaph engraved on the stone: *Faith, Purity,* and *Valor.* All three words in a neat, tidy row. Chimalis blanched and shook her head. There was no faith, purity, or valor in Lucas Maske's brittle bones. His soul had escaped his corpse, and he had devoured so many people that Chimalis felt nothing but rage, anger, and to be honest, a little fear. But she had to participate in this trance. She had no other choice.

"Really, Chimalis," Halian said as she logged into *Zoom* on her cell phone, "you're in a graveyard in the middle of the night?"

She nodded. "I need to be near Maske's grave to connect with him, to understand his life, so that I can find and kill him."

"But, you have no prayer sticks," Halian said. "No feathers or shells to make a cocoon around your body for protection."

"Yeah, but I do have a bowl of burning incense. That's sufficient." She crossed her legs on the quilt and settled into a comfortable position. "Come on, let's get going. We're wasting time here."

Before they began, Halian made it clear that he would not be responsible for any psychic damage that she experienced during the dream trance. He made her swear that she understood the repercussions. She did, just like she had sworn during her previous trance against El Cadejo.

"Okay, Chimalis," he said, "relax, close your eyes, breathe deeply, and follow my instructions."

Doing as he requested, she breathed deeply. She could smell the incense and hear crickets jabbering in the nearby woods. A car drove by the cemetery, its lights on, but she did not open her eyes to look at it, nor did she care. She wasn't concerned about passersby or anyone who might stop and investigate why she was in the middle of a cemetery with candles and incense. Both Luiz and Horus were in a car in the parking lot. If someone were to walk towards her, they'd intervene.

Halian spoke in Zuni, repeating incantations she had heard before. Soft, pleasant words. Words that set her mind at ease and calmed her spirit. In truth, she felt like lying down and taking a nap, but Halian's words carried her into a dream trance, and her mind opened to everything in Lucas Maske's past life.

A young child, born in the Penobscot Reservation Trust Land, not too far from Millinocket. A sweet boy, whose mother and father loved him and took care of him. Growing up quickly, making friends, confronting a few bullies, having difficulty with math in school, but always seeming to have an affection for medicine. He wanted to be a doctor; that seemed clear to Chimalis as his voice echoed through her mind.

Jump ahead several years. His father passed away from a heart condition. Lucas feels lost and distraught and cannot seem to cope in his high school years. His grades plummet as he struggles to graduate, but he passes by the proverbial "skin of his teeth" and enrolls in the Maine College of Health Professionals. There, he excels.

Chimalis opened her eyes, could smell the incense and hear Halian chant. She closed her eyes again and focused on Maske's medical career.

He became a cardiologist in the 1970's, one of the best Penobscot surgeons in Maine. For five years, he saved many lives, but always regretted that he could not save his father's life, though he tried on occasion to bring him back to life through incantation and Wabanaki ceremonials. He failed in those endeavors, and in time, heart procedures became tedious to him. So, he resigned from cardiology and settled for just being a primary care physician. Shortly thereafter, he became a chief surgeon.

A few years later, he met a woman, a nurse, who shared his devotion to medical care. They fell in love and married. She was Penobscot, like him, and in the five years that they were together, he couldn't imagine life without her.

She became pregnant. Five months later, she died from child-birth, as did his son, and Maske fell into such a deep malaise that he considered leaving the medical field. But he refused to do so, vowing to prevent any further suffering by his patients.

And that's when the killing started.

Elderly patients in hospice care. Secretly, he took them to his home, performed Algonquin rituals to soothe their suffering, and then either injected them with drugs that could not be detected through autopsy or cut their wrists and let them bleed out. He did it for them: to keep them from suffering brutal old age, from enduring their constant, agonizing pain. Men. Women. Even a few children. He felt that he was justified in his actions, that he was doing the "right thing."

Then, the police discovered his mercy killings. Gunfire ripped through his body, but he refused to die, and his spirit lifted up like a ball of light, into the canopy of trees near his home. His body died, but his spirit survived. And now he was Skadegamutc.

Chimalis placed her hands on the quilt, trying to feel her way to his coffin, seeking his bones so that she could divine his location. "Where are you?" She whispered. "Where are you?"

He had been all over Maine as the Skadegamutc, terrorizing not only the Wabanaki people, but Mainers as well. White people, descendants of those who had travelled across the Atlantic centuries ago to terrorize and enslave the Algonquin. The madness in his actions, his constant seeking of blood, and his persistent tap on sorrowful moments in peoples' memories to place them on the verge of death. He did all this for decades, and he could not stop.

*Where are you?*

Halian continued to chant, and Chimalis worked her way through incident after incident. All the devastation that the Skadegamutc had delivered to Maine, to Canada, and even to a few places in New Hampshire. Scores of bodies, scores of citizens who could no longer face their fears by committing suicide. She worked through every moment, even those that the beast had had with Niben Bellerose. Those were the worst for Chimalis, for she so loved and admired Niben for saving her life, that it was hard to witness, in dream state, Niben's abuse at the hands of the creature. Niben's death was even worse, and Chimalis, still in dream trance, almost passed out. But, she kept her spirit strong, struck her hand against the quilt, and channeled his bones to find his location.

She found him, lying on a cot, deep below a building. It was difficult to see where, for her mind was cluttered and confused with so many images of death. She drove her thoughts into the building, downstairs, down an escalator, and then into the room where the Skadegamutc seemed to be resting. Chimalis was quiet and careful not to rouse the beast from his deep sleep. She moved closer to the cot. Closer, closer...

There he was, on the cot, face up, and the room was cluttered with medical equipment, scalpels, knives, and forceps. She could smell chemicals, formaldehyde and sanitary fluids. He was lying there, eyes closed, his face savagely clawed by Joe Littlecloud during their deadly exchange. Chimalis hovered over the Skadegamutc, observing his face, his closed eyes, his deep grey flesh.

His eyes opened and Chimalis fell backward, into Maske's tombstone. Suddenly, she was out of dream trance.

Halian called to her. "Chimalis... are you all right?"

For a moment, she could not speak, short of breath, dizzy and confused. "I'm—I'm all right. I'm fine. Just a little dizzy."

Luiz and Horus ran across the graveyard and came to her. Luiz helped her up, keeping a tight grip on her shoulders. "Are you okay, boss? What did you see?"

She paused, cleared her throat, and said, "I found him, Luiz." She smiled. "I know where he is."

# CHAPTER FIFTEEN

*Millinocket Regional Hospital*

The Millinocket Regional Hospital wasn't far from Ferguson Lake: a little over a mile. Chimalis avoided looking at, or even thinking about that body of water. Now was the time to focus all her energy toward the Skadegamutc residing inside the facility.

But, where? Surely, the creature wasn't "hanging out" with patients or even the physicians or nurses working there, though the idea was probably appealing to it. It was somewhere inside, a place in secret, so that it could rest and recover from Joe Littlecloud's assault.

"How do we go in?" Horus asked as they sat in their rental car, watching the main entrance. Patients and emergency responders were going in and out. The sun was beginning to set. No time to waste.

"We go in like normal people," Chimalis said, "as if we're simply there to visit a patient."

"And what about this gasoline?" Luiz asked, holding up the can in the back seat. "Surely we can't just walk in with a can of gas."

Horus had brought the can in case it was necessary to use it, but stepping into a hospital with a can of flammable liquid would not sit well with the medical staff or the security personnel. Burning the creature alive was necessary, yes, but they simply couldn't waltz in with gasoline in their hands.

"Bring your lighters, but not the gas," Chimalis said. "We'll find something marked flammable in one of their labs. Now, let's go."

They climbed out of the car and walked toward the entrance. They nodded and smiled to the security officer standing beside the door. The glass doors opened, and they walked in. They ignored the receptionist at the front desk and walked down the hall lined with several patient rooms. Chimalis was concerned that the Skadegamutc could be feasting upon several of these patients, floating up into the hallway as a ball of light, and then shifting into human form. She had the desire to investigate every room and check every patient. But no. The creature was somewhere below the first floor.

*Somewhere.*

Through the dream trance in the graveyard, she had a notion as to where the creature was, but the location wasn't fully clear. The images were muddled and imprecise. The Skadegamutc had opened its eyes and peered at her through the dream. Chimalis hoped that the beast hadn't fled the hospital. *Unlikely*, she thought as they proceeded down the patient hallway. *What better place to kill us all than here?*

It was unlikely that the creature would kill them, though not impossible. Given the nature of its location underground and, presumably, in a small space, it could destroy them all.

As they walked down the hallway toward the elevator, Chimalis felt a surge of anxiety. Not the same kind of emotions that she had felt during the Thoreau-Wabanaki Trail Festival, but painful nonetheless. Her heart raced. She reached for her knife, but of course, the sheath was not on her belt. She had not brought it with her. It was in storage at the FBI office in Portland.

"We have to find some flammable liquid," Luiz said as they continued walking down the hallway.

Chimalis nodded. "Let's find the lab."

They followed the signs in the hallway leading to the laboratory. It was a small lab, with only one technician. They paused at the door. Chimalis tried opening it. It was locked.

She knocked. The lady in the lab turned and removed her glasses. Chimalis flashed her badge. "FBI," she said in a stern voice. "Open up, please."

"Why are you flashing your badge now?" Horus whispered in her ear.

Chimalis shook her head. "I've no choice. We've got to get in there."

That was true. They had not shown their badges to the receptionist because that would have caused security to follow them wherever they went, which could potentially cause the Skadegamutc to kill even more hospital personnel. Chimalis did not want to see that happen, but there was no choice now: the lab door was locked, and they needed to get in to find a flammable liquid.

The technician came to the door and swiped her badge against the identifier. The door unlocked and Chimalis walked in.

"What's going on?" The technician asked.

They flashed their badges again. Chimalis pointed to Horus and Luiz. "These are Agents Ruth and Vasquez. They need to ask you a few questions, please."

"About what?" the technician asked. "What's this all about?"

"Ma'am," Luiz said, eyeing Chimalis, "if you'll please step outside the lab, we'd like to ask you a few questions."

The tech hesitated, sighed, then walked out, leaving Chimalis in the room alone.

She searched the room. There were bottles of chemicals everywhere—Ethylene oxide, Hydrogen peroxide, Peracetic acid—scores of others. She opened cabinets along the wall. She searched for them all. Then, she found what she was looking for.

Chimalis smiled, grabbed the plastic bottle, tucked it into her coat pocket, and headed to the door. She opened the door, hearing the questions that Horus and Luiz were asking the technician. When they saw her, they stopped. "Thank you, ma'am," Horus said. "You may return to your lab. We've no further questions."

The lady was not happy with the interrogation. She glared at Chimalis as she pushed her way through the door and closed it again.

They went to the elevator. Luiz pushed the button, and they waited. "What did you get?" Horus asked.

Chimalis pulled the bottle out and showed it to them.

# CHAPTER SIXTEEN

"You do realize that Benzene is a carcinogen, right?" Horus asked. "It's not only highly flammable, but it can cause cancer."

"I'm well aware of that, sir," Chimalis said, putting the bottle back into her coat pocket, "but what other choice did I have? Benzene is flammable, as you say. You wanna kill the beast? We gotta use this chemical."

She was concerned about the chemical's fumes, which indeed, could cause cancer if ingested by a person nearby. They could all suck in the fumes and potentially die years later. But there were no other flammable chemicals in the lab. Benzene was the only option.

"Come on," she said, walking into the elevator. "Let's move. We don't have a lot of time."

The elevator door closed, and they went down to the bottom floor where the basement and parking garage were located. The door opened, and they stepped out, looking carefully through the dozens of parked vehicles, wondering where the Skadegamutc was located. Technically, the hospital did not have a basement per se, but it did have a few storage rooms where, presumably, medical equipment and other materials were stored. Chimalis walked to one of the rooms and tried opening the door. It was locked. They checked the second room. Also locked. The third was not locked, and Chimalis felt a tinge of anxiety in her mind.

"This is it," she said, her hand shaking a little. "This is where it is."

Luiz and Horus turned on the light in the third storage room. They walked in carefully, lighters in hand. But, there was no creature, no Skadegamutc anywhere among the boxes and crates. Horus moved to the back of the room, found a pile of crates against the wall, and pushed them aside. In the wall was a large hole, human-sized. Perfect for crawling through.

"This is where it is," Horus said, pointing through the hole. "The beast is down there."

The hole in the wall led to a long tunnel. Chimalis was reminded of the old movie *The Shawshank Redemption* as she crawled through it. She did not have anything tied to her foot like the main character in the film had, but it was a difficult crawl. Luckily, the tunnel did not lead to a sewage pipe; instead, it led to another room, all hollowed out. They climbed out of the tunnel and paused. Luiz clicked on his lighter and held it up, casting shadows on the walls and floor.

Bone fragments lay everywhere, and not all of them human. Chimalis could see bits of squirrel and rabbit bones. Clearly, the Skadegamutc had been in this tunnel system for quite a while. How often had it hidden here? Chimalis could not say. Joe Littlecloud certainly had no knowledge of the creature residing here. Obviously, Niben had diverted his attention away from the hospital.

"It feeds on animals too," Luiz said. "Interesting."

"There are human bones too," Chimalis said whispering, pointing at piles of dirt and white bone. "It probably came back here often to feed on patients." She crawled to another tunnel crudely etched out in the wall. "Come on, we've got to keep going."

"I'll lead," Horus said. "You guys follow."

Chimalis was concerned for Horus's safety. Putting himself in the lead could pose a serious risk, but Chimalis let him crawl into the tunnel first. She and Luiz followed.

Horus flicked on his lighter as he crawled through the tunnel, illuminating the passage and helping guide them into the next room. It wasn't a very long tunnel: Chimalis could see the hollowed-out space in front of them. Horus grabbed the edge of the passageway and pulled himself into the room.

The room had a coffin in the center on the dirt floor. A wooden coffin with warped slats on its sides and deep claws marks running its length. A wooden top rested on the coffin.

Horus touched the wooden top, perhaps trying to determine whether the Skadegamutc was in there or not. "We have to open it," he said, whispering. He looked at Chimalis. "Get your Benzene ready."

Chimalis wasn't so sure that the creature was in there. Maybe, maybe not. Nevertheless, she pulled out the plastic bottle from her coat, unscrewed the top, and waited.

Luiz stood at the top of the coffin, Horus at the bottom. They grabbed the top, and Luiz nodded. "Okay," he said, "one... two... three..."

They pulled the top off the coffin and let it fall to the floor. Chimalis doused the inside with Benzene. Luiz threw his lighter into the coffin. Flames erupted, but the Skadegamutc was not there, and the tattered cloth lay in ash.

"Damn!" Horus said. "Where the hell is it?"

A bright flash of light filled the room. Chimalis looked up to the ceiling as the Skadegamutc flew into Horus Ruth. Horus screamed, propelled across the room, and into the wall. Chimalis and Luiz fell backward at the sheer brilliance and power of the ball. Chimalis dropped her bottle.

She tried reaching for the Benzene again, the size of the bottle around 140 picometers, but the Skadegamutc shifted into human form. The beast was like a shadow, illuminated from the fire in the coffin. Chimalis turned and saw the creature move toward her.

Standing abnormally tall, the Skadegamutc crouched to keep from scraping his head against the ceiling. Chimalis backed away as his thin, dark grey arms reached for her, swiping out with claws at least two inches long. His face was taut, its mouth large. Its teeth were nothing but sharp, pointy fangs. His eyes were dark and bulbous. He wore a red cloak like the one burning in the coffin. He walked toward Chimalis with a maniacal grin on its face.

Luiz grabbed the bottle and tried splashing the creature with Benzene, but the Skadegamutc grabbed Luiz's throat, howled angrily, and tossed him over the burning coffin.

"Luiz!" Chimalis shouted. She tried crawling toward him, but the Skadegamutc wrapped her mind in chaos.

Again, images of her fiancé and his brutal death—the lacerations, the swelling, the broken bones—were clearer in her mind now than when she had tried drowning herself in Moosehead Lake. The details of his death, coupled with Luiz's injuries in Alaska and the painful images of her friends near death in Colorado, kept her locked in place, incapable of moving. She tried to crawl, tried reaching Luiz, but the memories were like handcuffs: she crawled toward the creature in front of her.

"You're in pain," the Skadegamutc said in a low, comforting voice, leaning over her as she huddled in fear. "I can feel your pain." He motioned toward her. "Come to me and let me ease your sorrow. I will save you from your suffering."

Chimalis felt a strong urge to go to him, to embrace him, and let him wash away her agony. But, she knew that that was what the creature did: console people whose minds he filled with pain. She wanted to go to him, but she resisted.

Behind the burning coffin, Chimalis could see Luiz recovering, preparing to attack the Skadegamutc and save her. But, that would be foolish, like what Niben had done to save her. If Luiz attacked, he would die, and Chimalis could not accept that.

She got an idea, a thought in her mind, separate from the painful memories of her past. One of the Skadegamutc's sorrows, one that she had seen during her dream trance. Chimalis kept thinking about it, again and again, projecting it out of her mind and into the beast's mind.

The Skadegamutc paused his comforting motions as the memories of his son dying, in painful agony like Chimalis's fiancé, filled his mind. His wife too, in this very hospital, incapable of surviving the birth. She threw the painful memories of his wife's and son's deaths at him, like thrusting her ceremonial knife into his heart. The creature stepped back, looking left, right, clearly trying to figure out what was wrong and how to cope. How could he possibly feel such anguish, such pain, when all his life he had filled his victims' minds with such sadness. How could he now feel those terrifying emotions himself?

The tragic memories of her past began to fade as she kept sending painful images into the Skadegamutc's mind. Behind the coffin, Luiz rose. Chimalis reached for the bottle of Benzene on the floor. She crawled to it and grabbed it. "Luiz!" she said, waving toward him. "The lighter!"

The Skadegamutc continued backing away. It appeared fuzzy, as if it were trying to shift into a ball of light. Luiz threw his lighter to Chimalis. Chimalis flung the Benzene toward the Skadegamutc, splashing its red clothing. She flicked on the lighter and tossed it at the beast.

The Skadegamutc screamed as flames leeched up its pants and set its legs and arms on fire. It roared, its voice so piercing that Chimalis covered her ears. It continued to burn, and burn, and burn. It tried again to shift into a ball of light, but the fire kept it from changing. The creature roared again, tried reaching for Chimalis, but it fell, its legs shattering into a pile of ash and dust. Its arms did the same. It fell forward, face first, onto the ground. It tried moving again, to shift again, but it couldn't. The fire coursed through its chest, into its face, and finally, into its mind. It lay there burning, while the coffin nearby burned as well, two fires in what Chimalis considered the end.

Five minutes later, the Skadegamutc was nothing but a pile of black ash. It was gone.

Chimalis, recovering from those painful memories, stood carefully. Luiz joined her. He gave her a strong side hug. "You did great, boss," he said. "You're the best."

Against the wall, Horus stirred. Chimalis was relieved. He wasn't dead. That, at least, was a blessing.

She went to him and helped him sit. "Are you all right?" She asked.

Horus nodded, rising, rubbing his sore neck. "I'm fine, thank you. And thank you, Chimalis. Luiz is right: you *are* the best."

She waved them off and then stood there, looking at the burning pile of ash. "What do we do now?" Luiz asked.

Chimalis stared at it, afraid to even touch it. Could it, again, fill her mind with horrible images? Could it re-form back into a Skadegamutc and continue to terrorize the sweet people of Maine? A Penobscot wizard, it was said, could never die. Was that correct?

*Maybe*, she thought. *Just Maybe.*

"I know what to do with it," Horus said. "I know."

# CHAPTER SEVENTEEN

Chimalis held the black urn out the car window. She tipped it carefully, letting the Skadegamutc's ashes fly backward. A cloud of grey dust, drifting in the wind and falling to the ground. Chimalis smiled. She was having a good time.

Luiz was fine. The Skadegamutc had knocked him over the coffin, but he had no serious damage, no deep lacerations, no broken bones. He did have a few burns on his body from passing through the fire, but Luiz was, thankfully, driving the car while Chimalis spread the creature's ashes across Maine. Horus, unfortunately, suffered a few serious injuries. He had a concussion and a couple of broken ribs. Ironically, he was convalescing at the Millinocket Regional Hospital, right where the Skadegamutc had tried to recover. But overall, Horus was fine. He'd be up and ready to go soon, and Chimalis wondered if perhaps he'd be willing to help her in her VPA duties.

She looked over at Luiz and smiled again. Luiz was the best, but it never hurt to have an extra hand to aid in her pursuit of Native American cryptids.

Chimalis dipped the urn again and let the final clump of ashes float away. Then, she tossed the urn into the ditch on the side of the road. It was over. The Skadegamutc's ashes had been strewn across ten miles of road. It would never, ever rise again.

Her cell phone rang. She looked at the screen. It was SAC Halsey. Chimalis swiped right and put the phone to her ear.

"Good morning, Special Agent Halsey," Chimalis said. "What's the good word?"

Halsey cleared his throat and said, *"The good word is that you've been cleared of all criminal charges. The FBI has determined that you were not responsible for the deaths of those FBI agents in Alaska. Congratulations."*

Chimalis paused, then, "Thank you, Agent Halsey. I'm glad to hear it."

"You're welcome. Now, I need you back in Denver as soon as possible. The VPA is in need of your services."

She hung up, and Luiz asked, "You've been cleared?"

Chimalis nodded.

"Congratulations, boss."

Chimalis acknowledged Luiz's remarks, but she turned to the car window and stared out into the thick woods on the side of the road.

"Are you thinking about resigning?" Luiz asked.

She wanted to respond, but she couldn't. The idea of remaining in the VPA troubled her. She had to go to New Mexico and get her knife fixed; that was a given. But, all her emotions, her fears, and her psychological trauma were, right now, still prominent in her mind. They were difficult to shake.

"You're the best agent we've got," Luiz said. "No one is better than you."

Chimalis appreciated the compliment, but still wasn't sure of her decision. There were other agents in the VPA that were quite competent in their duties. Luiz was one, for sure. She turned to him and was about to speak.

"And you know," he said, interrupting, "I've received reports of Mannegishi causing great trouble to the Cree Nation in Canada." Luiz shrugged. "We could go there and check it out. What do you say?"

The Mannegishi? The so-called "little people" of the Cree who would climb out of the rocks on the side of rivers and capsize canoes, drowning folks. She had heard offhand reports of at least three people being drowned by these little "tricksters." Their deaths infuriated her.

Stay or resign? *I've no other choice*, she thought, finally making her decision. *I must serve the VPA… forever.*

"Fine," Chimalis said, feeling annoyed, but happy at the same time. "We'll go and get those mean little creatures."

She pulled out her knife and looked at it. Still cracked, and pulsing blue light. She rolled it around in her hand, observing the cryptid icons on the blade... and Joe Littlecloud's icon split in two. "But first, we need to fix this knife, and then we'll head to Canada." She pointed in the direction of the airport. "Drive on, Luiz. Our duty awaits!"

"Yes, sir, boss," Luiz said with a broad smile.

# ABOUT THE AUTHOR

Robert E. Waters is a technical writer by trade, but has been a science fiction/fantasy fan all his life. He's worked in the computer and board gaming industry since 1994 as designer, producer, and writer. In the late 90's, he tried his hand at writing fiction, and since 2003, has sold over seven novels and eighty stories to various on-line and print magazines and anthologies, including the *Grantville Gazette*, Eric Flint's online magazine dedicated to publishing stories set in the 1632/Ring of Fire Alternate History series.

Robert's first 1632/Ring of Fire novel, *1636: Calabar's War*, (co-authored with Charles E Gannon), was recently published by Baen Books. Robert has also co-written several 1632 stories, including the *Persistence of Dreams* (Ring of Fire Press), with Meriah L Crawford, and *The Monster Society*, with Eric S Brown.

Robert is the author of *The Mask Cycle*, a Baroque fantasy series which includes the novels *The Masks of Mirada* and *The Thief of Cragsport* (Ring of Fire Press).

For e-Spec Books, Robert has written several stories which have appeared in the widely popular military science fiction anthology series, *Defending the Future*. All seven of his stories which appeared in the series were recently collected into one volume titled *Devil Dancers*.

Robert currently lives in Baltimore, Maryland with his wife Beth and their son Jason.

*artist's rendition of a Skadegamutc*

## SKADEGAMUTC

*(Also known as Ghost Witch)*

ORIGINS: This is a blood-sucking creature from the lore of the Wabanaki, also called People of the Dawnland, an alliance of tribes located in Maine that still exist today. It is said that those who practice black magic come back after death as this type of vampire, though contrary to other vampire lore, they do not retain a healthy, youthful appearance, instead showing the decay of death.

DESCRIPTION: During the daylight hours the ghost witch appears as one would expect a corpse to look, with flesh that is decaying or desiccated and that shows evidence of any injuries that lead to their death. At night they transform to a glowing orb that travels through the darkness looking for humans to prey upon. By some accounts they can transform back to their zombie state and feed. To maintain their existence they must consume flesh and blood. They are said to retain their magical abilities and are reported to cast curses on those they encounter. They have two ways they typically attack. The first is to prey on the grief-stricken, hovering near open-air burials waiting for the mourners to rest, which is when they strike. The second is to fly around looking for travelers who have been separated from their group. When they find them, they swoop down and quietly feed.

In their undead form they cannot be harmed, except if burned to ash and the remains scattered.

LIFE CYCLE: As this cryptid results from the death of a practitioner of black magic, it cannot be said to have a life cycle, but sorcerers who refuse to stay dead come back as this creature.

HISTORY: Among the tribes there are stories of those who encountered this creature, notably one couple traveling through the woods who chose to shelter in a grove where a magician had been put to rest in the trees. Despite the wife's reluctance, they bedded down beneath the trees for the night. The wife woke to a gnawing sound that had disturbed her sleep all night. When she went to wake her husband his left side had been eaten away, including his heart. She went to the townfolk for help. When she told her horrific story, they lowered the magician's corpse to discover blood on its face.

# ABOUT THE ARTIST

Until his decades-long disappearance, JW Harp was known for his trippy underground comic strip *Captain Thetan*, about a seafarer who controls reality for himself and others. This otherworldly character appeared in a dozen issues of the classic rare underground zine *Sandanista Romp*. JW has reemerged thanks largely to eSpec Books' Systema Paradoxa series. In 2023, JW started Skilletfire Studios with comic-book author Scott Eckelaert. Under the Skilletfire Studios mantle, JW has produced the graphic novel *Boylon Heights*, and the *Gimme Five Comics* series. Since its launch, *Gimme Five Comics* has included work by Artyom Topilin, Elena Cerisciola, John L. French, Keith Lansdale, and Joe R. Lansdale with more to come.

JW grew up in the seedy parts of South Carolina, which is all of it. He feels part Canadian and part Costa Rican these days. He lives in North Carolina. Please get in touch with him at jwharp@skilletfire.com.